Love
forever ❤
@
Rajpath

Approved........ As proposed

Kalpana Mishra

Srishti
PUBLISHERS & DISTRIBUTORS

Srishti Publishers & Distributors
Registered Office: N-16, C.R. Park
New Delhi – 110 019
Corporate Office: 212A, Peacock Lane
Shahpur Jat, New Delhi – 110 049
editorial@srishtipublishers.com

First published by
Srishti Publishers & Distributors in 2016

Dedicated to the two most important men in my life:
One who shaped me and made me
The person that I am today
My late grandfather Shri D.P. Tejwani;
The other without whose unconditional support
My life would not have been what it is today
My late father-in-law Shri Gopal Mishra.

Acknowledgements

As I keep my fingers crossed that this book is liked and enjoyed by all, I also hope that it may become a source of creating awareness amongst our countrymen and women.

My parents: Thank you for making me what I am today.

My husband, Shailendra Kumar Mishra: I can't thank you enough for first conceiving the idea of creating this work of fiction, and for keeping patience enough – even when I used to lose it and wanted you to leave everything aside too. You not only lend your ears to what I had penned down, but gave your earnest opinion too.

My kids: I wish to thank my kids who were five years old and one year old then. Especially my daughter, who being the elder one used to play and babysit her newborn sibling when I wished to pen down some ideas immediately.

My friends Hemlata, Monika, Lakshmi and Reema: The book would not have been completed had my friend Hemlata not stood behind me like a rock, coaxing me to write further. I wish to thank my best friend Monika for taking out precious time from her busy schedule and becoming my first editor-in-chief. I had constant discussions with the four of them through various phases of drafting and re-drafting, and coming up with a suitable title and a cover page for the book. I also wish to thank all those who helped me in editing the script and making it crisper.

Lokesh and Prateek: Thanks to my photographer Lokesh and the book cover designer Prateek for using their craft so precisely to give the book the look that it so rightly deserved.

Srishti Publishers: It was the logo of the publishing house that caught my attention so much that I actually wished secretly that this book be selected by them for publication. They turned out to be a real source of inspiration.

Special credits: Special thanks to Aastha, Umesh and Palak for being my continuous support systems.

Although planned as a work of fiction, as I completed the writing part, I realised that this book has a few resemblances with my real life too. Hence, I take this opportunity to thank all the people who have been a part of my life's journey so far.

In the end, I wish to thank the Government of India for introducing Child Care Leave (CCL), which helped me in tending to my newborn and grooming my elder one during their formative years. I actually felt rewarded when my daughter (seven years now) came up with her own short story one fine day. Hoping to see her write many more.

Prologue

It was like any other day in Patiala House Court in Delhi when Shalini entered. She was nervous as hell. She had accompanied her superiors to the court for defending official cases earlier too, but this was the first time on two accounts: firstly, she had come to file a case and not defend it; secondly, this time it was her personal case.

The chances of one filing a case against a loved one are rare. Such a decision is not made at the drop of a hat. Anyone who has been through it would have definitely felt the pain and agony and gone through the turmoil, the way Shalini was going through. She felt like Arjuna from the *Mahabharata,* who had to fight a war against his own people. But, at that point of time, she was sure of what she was doing; that she wanted to teach him a lesson.

Sitting there on a bench, and waiting for her turn to come, she was going through thousands of emotions. Being aware that this case may bring about an end to her relationship with Kartik, she was secretly hoping that her fears may prove to be false. Ignoring the fact that Kartik had not spoken to her even once since the time she had taken the decision to file the case, she was just being confident of the man in her life. Hoping blissfully that he might be reeling under the initial shock, but would soon be back with her and supporting her as always. Little was she aware of the impact of family bonding and pressures that Kartik was going through.

Case numbers were being called from the court room, and Shalini's case was still a few numbers away. Half an hour later, her number was called, Case No. 24. At that moment, she felt that here in this place, her whole identity had probably been huddled to a case number. Her advocate took her inside the room from where the number was called. The court room was not the same as is seen in the Hindi movies. It was much less crowded than the waiting area outside that she had just witnessed. It seemed to her that the woes of the people present inside were written all over their faces. Although, as the judge was about to give his verdict in the case preceding hers, it was already clear from the looks on the faces of the parties involved whose favour it was going to be in.

The judge then asked for the next complainant. After having heard the case through the advocate first and Shalini later, the judge asked, "Who is there from the defendant's side?"

Suddenly she went numb upon seeing Kartik entering through the door.

"I am representing the defendant," said Kartik, leaving Shalini in a state of shock, unable to understand whether this actually meant *an end to her most loved relationship.*

"**K**artik, come let's go and meet our new batch-mates," said Shyamal Kumar. He had been the second person from the 2000 batch to join the organization in 2002. He had joined the post of Assistant, a Group B post in a ministry of the Government of India. Kartik had been the first one to join. All employees in a ministry are categorised under Groups from A to D, A being the highest rank.

Kartik Vats, a tall, fair-complexioned twenty-six-year-old guy, had a thick moustache and was soft spoken. It had been barely a month since Kartik had been appointed and had joined the Finance Department. But this young and dynamic man, who was otherwise an introvert, was already considered an outstanding performer. He requested Shyamal to wait for him, as he had to finish something.

Five minutes later, he appeared from his room to find Shyamal waiting for him patiently. Both of them went to meet the new appointees who were eager to get their first appointment. A girl was sitting quietly in a corner amidst the bunch of ten boys.

Suddenly everyone became alert when the dealing clerk issued the second list of new appointees to attend a five-day compulsory departmental training. Shyamal and Kartik, more experienced by virtue of their date of joining, got the list; the first name to be called out was Shyamal's.

He asked Kartik why his name was not on the list. Kartik sadly informed him that his was on the first list. "Wish I was in this batch."

They were immediately surrounded by their new colleagues, eager to know whether their names were on the list or not. The office, which so far had been as quiet as a mortuary, suddenly sounded like a Class I classroom.

Kartik quickly took charge of the situation and declared the names of the appointees on the list. Everyone concerned was to report to the training room.

He read out the names fast and reached the only female name: Shalini Pahilajani. He glanced at her. Wearing a yellow kurta and red salwar with a red and yellow dupatta, she was approximately five-foot-one-inch tall and wore spectacles on her oval-shaped face. Upon hearing her name, she immediately said thanks and went out, as did the others. Kartik bid adieu to Shyamal and returned to his section.

The training room had two-seater benches. By the time Shyamal reached the room, all the others had made themselves comfortable. Shalini, who was always a frontbencher, sat in the front. The seat next to her was empty and Shyamal sat down.

The training began. The lecturers were seniors working in the Department, and they introduced themselves and asked the trainees to do the same.

"My name is Shalini Pahilajani," Shalini introduced herself when her turn came. "I have worked in the Bikaner Bank Housing Finance Limited (BB HFL) as a Recovery Officer for two years."

Shyamal introduced himself after that. He had worked for five years as an accountant in another government department. It appeared that it was a mixed batch, comprising assistants, clerks and stenographers. They were informed that a ministry is basically created to assist the concerned minister in the formulation of various government policies. They were told about their job roles in the organization.

During lunch, Shalini sat alone, so Shyamal invited her to sit with him as he was also eating alone. Both of them discussed that day's lectures. They had just finished when Kartik appeared. He wished both of them. Shalini gestured with her hand as if to say hello, but Kartik did not take his hands out of his pockets. Shalini felt embarrassed and immediately looked away. Although she came from a middle class family, her job at BBHFL had made her outspoken and frank.

Shyamal hailed from Bihar, was married, and had two daughters. He was well-behaved, very talkative, witty and loved food. He had noticed Kartik's reaction and after a while took him outside and asked the reason for it.

"You have also been working in a government organization for the past five years; you should know that people of all ages work here. They don't even need a reason to create a mountain out of a molehill, especially the older ones. My reaction to her hello will make her think twice the next time," said Kartik.

◆

All the new appointees attended the lectures conscientiously. At the end of the five-day training session, all of them collected in the HR-1 Department which was responsible for issuing the posting orders. However, it turned out that the director who was to take the final decision about the postings of the new appointees was on leave for three days. The newbies would have to wait.

The first day passed. All the new entrants went to meet their friends in the department, and people from outside Delhi took permission and went sightseeing. However, Shalini was a Delhiite and did not want to go out, so the day was rather a boring one for her.

The next day, she had made up her mind not to spend the entire day sitting idle. Early in the morning, she went straight to the HR-1 Department and looked for somebody who could help her out. She was greeted by Sunaina, a young lady in her thirties.

"Yes, how may I help you?" asked Sunaina.

"Ma'am, kindly give me some work to do. I cannot sit idle."

"But, I cannot give you any work since your posting has not been decided yet. This section comprises confidential work. I hope you understand that now, that is, after your training."

Shalini insisted that in that case, she be allowed to go home promising to return as soon as the posting was decided. As if she knew what the lady was going to ask next, she added after a pause that she wished to finalise her subjects for the Civil Services Exam for CSE-2003.

"Oh! So you are a civil service aspirant! The next thing you will request me is to give you a lighter section, so that you can study in the office too, isn't it?"

Shalini sensed the sarcasm in her tone. Nonetheless, she stood her ground firmly. "No Ma'am, if that was the case, why would have I requested you to give me some work in the first place?"

Sunaina thought about it for a moment and agreed to give her a diary and dispatch work. Shalini agreed excitedly.

"Oh, so you seem to be excited about it. But during your training you must have been told that it is the job of an LDC, who is two ranks junior to you," Sunaina said, trying to assess Shalini's temperament.

"Ma'am, what I have learnt during the training was theoretical knowledge, but I have yet to get hands-on training. If I don't know my junior's job well, why would they look up to me for advice? I think this would be good exposure before joining any section. I hope I am allowed to do it for two days or so, till we get our posting order." Shalini was confident. Hearing this, Sunaina got up from her seat completely impressed and introduced Shalini to the dispatch clerk.

Two days later, Shalini and Shyamal both got postings in that very building; they were posted in the HR and Finance Department, respectively. The rest were sent away to various other departments located in different buildings. After getting his posting, Shyamal went directly to Kartik's room and informed him about it. Both of them felt happy that they will now be able to catch up during their lunch hours. Shyamal told him about the lectures, the security briefing, and so on. Kartik eagerly waited for Shyamal to tell him about Shalini's posting. But that was not meant to be.

Kartik listened to everything patiently for half an hour, but when he could not take it any longer, he reminded Shyamal politely that he has already been through the one week in-house training module and that he was interested in the postings of the rest of the trainees. From his expression, however, Shyamal understood the exact meaning of the question he had asked. Shyamal told him about everybody's posting, except for one person's. This irritated Kartik further. Suddenly he got a call from his room and left. He started his work but was unable to concentrate for the rest of the day. Hailing from a humble background in Bihar, he stayed with his younger brother in Delhi. That day after work, he thought about Shalini all the way home.

The next day, he started early and went straight to HR-1 first and asked for the list of new appointees. He found out that she had been posted in HR-2. She must be good, he thought, as only the best were appointed to HR. He quickly gave the list back and went to his room.

Shalini joined her section in HR-2, introduced herself and was welcomed by everyone. She started learning about her job and immersed herself in her work with dedication and enthusiasm. The work culture and the infrastructure were in complete contrast to those at her previous job. Although the infrastructure was good, the way the sarkari babus kept their files gave the office a shabby look. Sometimes she found it irritating that some basic facilities which had been available to everyone at her previous job were rationed here in accordance with the ranks of the officers and staff. Nonetheless, she tried to settle into the new environment amicably.

A few days later, Shalini got a call on her section's intercom from Sunaina Narain, the senior assistant posted in HR-1. Sunaina asked Shalini to have lunch with them that day, as they were having a small party. Although Shalini was an extrovert, she was slow at making genuine friends. She knew that this could be her chance to get to know new people. That day, she did not drive down to BBHFL, something she used to do during most of her lunch hours.

At one o'clock, she went to HR-1 and was greeted by five ladies almost ten or twelve years older than her. Shalini greeted all of them. As soon as she had made herself comfortable, Sunaina asked Shalini her zodiac sign. Shalini was taken aback as this was one question she had resolved that she would not ask anybody; she wanted to get rid of such superstitions. Shalini took a long time to answer Sunaina's simple question. She knew what the next question would be if she took more time; and there it was, "Tell me your date of birth and I shall tell you your zodiac sign."

Choosing to ignore Sunaina's second question so as not to appear like a newbie, Shalini immediately replied that she was a Piscean. Sunaina exclaimed in excitement that even she was a Piscean. When they exchanged their dates of birth, Sunaina replied with even greater enthusiasm, telling Shalini that she was exactly ten years and one day older than her.

Shalini realized the striking similarities between the two of them. She finally had a new friend – Sunaina Narain – her first one at her new job. She also got to know that Sunaina was very hard working and was considered the best in the whole of the HR department. She started going to Sunaina's room very often during lunch time.

During one such meeting, Sunaina told Shalini that the moment she had said that she wanted to have some work because she couldn't sit idle, that very moment they had decided to post her in HR-2. She informed her that they were getting good reports about her and assured Shalini of her guidance in case of any problems. Within a month of associating with each other, Shalini had already started looking up to Sunaina as a guide and mentor, while Sunaina affectionately called Shalini her prodigy.

Shalini informed Sunaina that she had decided on her subject for the CSE 2003, "I wonder if you'd know where can I get good books on public administration or PA."

"The office library houses some good books. You can also give a requisition for the books you need, if they are not available," replied Sunaina.

Shalini ventured into the office library to look for books on Public Administration. A few people were standing near the bookshelves, while some were at the reading table skimming through newspapers and magazines. Many of them were snoring at the table – a scene common in any office library. Shalini was busy looking for relevant books when she heard a male voice say hello. She looked behind and saw Kartik smiling at her. She smiled back but continued with her task.

Kartik came close and whispered, "What books are you looking for?"

She replied unwillingly, "Books on PA."

Kartik had thought that many people, especially women, who joined a government organization as assistants stopped trying to advance their careers further, but she was not like the others; she was different.

Shalini asked him if he was also trying for the civil services. Without a second thought, he immediately said yes.

"Oh, what are your subjects?"

"My subjects...eh...hmm..."

He pretended to be busy, looking for some books.

"I have taken up PA," she continued without waiting for his reply.

"Oh! That's my subject too," exclaimed Kartik, his loud voice making a few eyebrows go up. They decided to go out and talk.

As they chatted, the two of them discovered that they had done their honours in Mathematics. Shalini felt an academic connection.

"What books are you looking for?" he asked.

"A book on PA written by M. Laxmikanth."

"I have that book and I don't think it's available here."

"It is supposed to be the Bible for PA students. You should go through that book well. I think I should place a requisition for it."

"A requisition?" Kartik laughed loudly.

"Why are you laughing? What is the problem?"

Kartik controlled himself and informed her that by the time she got the book from the library, the CSE 2003 would have already been conducted.

"Oh! Does it take that long? But I was told that..." She was not able to complete her sentence when Kartik said, "Never mind,

Shalini. I have read that book and now I am going through some other books on the subject. If you want, I can lend it to you."

"Oh, that's so nice of you. It is an expensive book. I am planning to buy it as soon as I get my next salary. Till then, if you can lend me the book, I would be obliged," she replied.

Both of them went back to work. That day Kartik reached home late. His younger brother Dheeraj was waiting for him, "What is the matter, Bhaiya? You are so late today."

"Oh, nothing, just went to buy a book from Jawahar Book Depot," replied Kartik.

Jawahar Book Depot was a book shop in the crowded Ber Sarai Market, famous for books for the civil services examinations. All civil services aspirants, whether they lived in Delhi or otherwise, definitely visited Jawahar Book Depot and the other book shops in Ber Sarai Market, at least once during the course of their preparation.

Kartik told his brother that he had decided to start preparations for the CSE 2003.

"But you had told me that you were satisfied with your current job. What is the reason behind this sudden change in decision?"

On seeing a despondent look on his brother's face, Kartik asked, "Don't you think we all should keep trying for something better?"

"Bhaiya, I am happy for you, but worried for my own career. I know when you start your CSE preparation, you will not be able to concentrate on anything else. Right now, I am almost twenty-four years old, a simple graduate. It could seem to be selfish of me but I feel that it is me who requires your time and help to prepare for a government job, so that Ma and Pitaji can finally be free of their responsibilities."

Kartik was listening patiently when suddenly he heard Dheeraj sobbing. He took a deep breath and told Dheeraj to come and sit beside him. Dheeraj obeyed dutifully.

Kartik spoke with a mix of politeness and firmness, "You know, I have been dreaming of you getting a government job soon. It is only your hard work that can make you an achiever. As far as my help is concerned, rest assured, not a single day will pass when I will not be sitting with you for an hour to solve your problems or for taking tests as it has always been. Your examinations and career will be our priorities."

Dheeraj smiled. They decided to take a test at 10.00 p.m. sharp. Kartik and Dheeraj had three elder brothers and one elder sister. Kartik was the fifth and Dheeraj the sixth and the youngest child in the family. Although Dheeraj was only two years younger, Kartik treated him like his own child.

After freshening up, Kartik sat at his study table and spotted the book, the one he had promised to give to Shalini. He looked at the book and thought about Shalini. "She is so focused; she spoke to me only about the CSE. There is something in her that is not allowing me to concentrate on anything else. What is it that has caught my attention and is making me think about her? Why did I buy such an expensive book only to give it to her, while I have not even thought which subject I will take up for the CSE?"

He was suddenly woken up from his thoughts by Dheeraj who was calling him to take the test.

The next day Shalini entered her room and found Kartik waiting for her. She kept her bag down as Kartik greeted her. "Here is your book," he said.

Both of them decided to go to the canteen while the sweeper was cleaning the room. Shalini was venturing into the office canteen for the first time and found that it was chaotic. It seemed like all the older people had turned into college students in the canteen. Kartik and Shalini settled down and ordered some tea. Shalini was going through the book; suddenly she noticed that some of the pages were glued together, as if they had never been opened. She enquired about it and Kartik thought fast to find a suitable answer.

"I am yet to read that chapter, as it was not very important," he replied.

Although Shalini looked sceptical, she chose to stay mum. While she was going through the book, Kartik watched her carefully from the other end of the small canteen table, as if trying to assess the reasons that made him think about her. All the while he was also careful that neither Shalini nor anyone else around caught him gazing at her.

Shalini had a broad forehead with a small kumkum tika near her eyebrows where women generally put their bindi. She wore small framed spectacles over her big eyes and her small, hanging earrings were beautiful too. He felt there was something that made her different from the other girls who were the same age as her. What was it? Kartik was deeply engrossed in his own world when suddenly Shyamal put his hand on his friend's shoulder.

"Good morning, Shyamal. Come sit down," blurted Kartik who was clearly stunned. Shalini also looked up from her book and greeted Shyamal quickly. Kartik looked at his watch and rose to find out why their tea was taking such a long while to be served.

Shyamal told them that the canteen staff did not have much time in the morning and they had to provide room service as well. The government ensured that employees' needs were met in their rooms itself to ensure a greater output. However, if one still wished to come to the canteen, everything would be available, but only at the counter.

"Then, why do we still see such a crowd in the canteen all the time?" asked Kartik inquisitively.

"Because room service is provided only once in the morning and once in the afternoon, while people like me may feel hungry any time of the day."

Kartik applauded his frankness and came back with a tray of tea and samosas.

Shyamal exclaimed, "Wow! How do you know that I wanted a samosa too?"

"Your tummy told me, you fatty." And all of them laughed together.

Kartik went back to his room and thought that he has never looked at any woman so closely and intently. Still he was unable to figure out what it was about her that was holding his attention. He suddenly looked at his files and was reminded of the pending work on his table. He quickly had a sip of water and refreshed himself for the day's work.

Two days later, during lunch break, Kartik was reading the newspaper in the library when he saw Shalini going out of it. "When did she enter the library? I must have been so engrossed in the article that I missed her. How will I contact her now and on what pretext? Should I ask her about her preparation?"

He thought of going to her room, but went to his own room instead. He had just sat down in his chair when his section officer called him saying there was a call for him. There was an intercom for internal calls in every section and an MTNL landline which had been installed for incoming or outgoing calls. Usually, both the landline and intercom phones were kept on the table for the Section Officer or SO.

Kartik thought it was probably Shyamal on the intercom as usual. He said, "Hello," hastily and heard a female respond.

"Oh, hello Shalini." Trying to hide his excitement, he greeted her.

"Just saw you in the library. You were busy so did not want to bother you. I wanted to talk to you about two things."

I would have been happy to be bothered by you at any hour of the day, he thought.

"Are you there?"

"Oh! Yes I am very much here," Kartik replied and paid attention so he could listen to her two-point agenda.

Shalini told him that she had photocopied the chapters she required and wanted to return his book.

"What is the second point?"

"Yeah, wanted to discuss the circular on Hindi *Pakhwada*."

It is a fifteen-day celebration to promote the usage of hindi language in government organizations through various competitions like debates, talks, poetry recitation competitions, etc.

"I have not seen the circular. What is it about?"

Shalini became excited and said that a *vaak pratiyogita*, a debate on a given topic would be organised during the Pakhwada.

He asked her hesitantly if she could come to the canteen at four and tell him all about it. She refused politely because she had some work, and asked if they could discuss it over the intercom itself. Kartik said that since he had not seen the circular he was not in a position to comment on it.

"Then let's talk about it tomorrow during lunch in the canteen," said Shalini. He agreed delightedly.

Shalini felt pleased after the conversation. It was not that she had so much work that she could not have moved out even for five minutes. However, she was hesitant in going out at a time other than lunch time.

On the other hand, Kartik was equally satisfied that he had found a way to meet her again. The next day, Kartik was about to leave for the canteen when he realized that meeting Shalini all alone would not be a good idea. So he first went to Shyamal's room and brought him along. Shalini, too, quickly finished her lunch to reach the canteen in time.

Kartik and Shyamal were already waiting for her. She placed the circular on the table and took her seat. The boys read it. Before Kartik could say anything, Shyamal looked at Kartik angrily and asked him, "What was so urgent about this circular that you didn't allow me to have my lunch? The circular is in every room."

Shalini quickly asked, "Why did you not have your lunch?"

Kartik thanked the heavens that she had not realized that the circular was in every room. However, he thought it would be prudent to divert Shyamal's attention to something else. He took just a second to think about what it could be.

"Shyamal, why don't you get today's special dish for yourself from the canteen so that you can have it with your lunch. It will certainly be my treat."

Kartik's idea proved to be good bait.

As soon as Shyamal left, Shalini asked Kartik if he was participating as well because, as she was new, she was afraid of being the only one. She also told him that she had asked everyone in both HR-2 and HR-1, but no one was willing to participate.

"I am afraid I cannot say yes as I have stage fright," informed Kartik hesitantly. Shalini had not been expecting such an answer. She tried to persuade him, but could not. Kartik knew that she must have felt bad, so he assured her that he would be present to support her during the event. "But, I want to know why are you so eager to take part in the vaak pratiyogita?

"Both my parents are government servants and they used to show me these Hindi Pakhwada circulars when they were organized in their respective organizations. However, due to stage fright, they never participated in such competitions. I want to do it for them."

Kartik wished her all the very best. Suddenly, they were distracted by a loud burp. Shyamal said jokingly that his tummy was thanking Kartik.

Shalini promised herself that even if none of her batch-mates agreed to participate, she would definitely take part in the competition.

However, sometimes, what you plan is not what is destined to be.

It was the 20th of August 2002. All the employees had taken the pledge for Sadhbhawana Diwas. The day was celebrated to commemorate the birth anniversary of Rajiv Gandhi. When Shalini reached home, her father's best friend, Mahinder Uncle and his wife had come to pay a visit. Shalini looked up to them and respected them. Mahinder Uncle used to take great interest in her professional life and guided her wherever required.

However, this time it was something different. Shalini went to sit with them in the drawing room. Her mother asked her to make some tea and papad for them and Shalini obeyed her.

After a while, her mother came into the kitchen and informed her that Aunty had come with a proposal for her.

"What proposal?"

Shalini could tell there was a problem.

"A marriage proposal. He is a CA," her mother said in a single breath.

This was not a problem; it was more like a bomb blast. She went blank and could not utter a word. "What a day to choose – the day of harmony." She felt that all the harmony in her life had vanished into thin air.

Mahinder Uncle and Aunty did not have any child. Hence, they treated Shalini like their own and were very affectionate towards her. They told them that the CA was one of Aunty's relatives' son.

"Shalini, the tea is boiling. Switch off the gas and bring it to the drawing room. I am taking the papad with me," her mother said but Shalini was lost in her own world.

Her mother could already sense that Shalini would not be able to say anything at that moment. She had also not wanted to discuss the subject with Shalini in Mahender Uncle and Aunty's presence.

While pouring the tea in the cups in the kitchen, Shalini wanted to cry. She wished that Uday, her younger brother, was there with her. Still, she mustered some courage to go out, lest the tea got cold. She went out with the tea and was greeted by both Uncle and Aunty.

"Do you know, Shalini, there is a saying amongst Sindhis; one who starts preparing good papad is ready for marriage. So, I think this is the most opportune moment. Think about it, beta," said Uncle warmly.

At any other moment, she would have taken the joke with good humour, but not that day. Her eyes were brimming with tears, so she simply got up and left the room. Just like most elders, everyone thought that Shalini was feeling shy and that is why she had left.

Later in the night, after dinner, Shalini lay down, but was unable to sleep. She got up and called Uday, who was more of a friend for her. He was working in a call centre. Due to the timings of his job, they met only on the weekends. She wanted to tell him about Uncle's visit. However, he already knew everything and was very happy for her. She told him hesitantly that she did not want to get married. Uday was now worried and asked her the reason for her refusal. He was certain that his sister was not seeing anyone.

At that moment, her mother came and kept her hand on Shalini's head affectionately. Shalini disconnected the call and hugged her mother tightly. Tears began rolling down her cheeks. Both of them sat on the bed. Her mother gave her a glass of water. She asked Shalini to tell her honestly what the matter was and if she had somebody else in mind.

"Mamma no, that's not the case. You know all my friends. I have never hidden anything from you. It's just that I do not want to get married," replied Shalini, still in a pensive mood.

"Your father and I have always given priority to a good education and profession before marriage. Now you have achieved both. Above all, you are already twenty-four. You know I got married when I was your age," her mother explained.

"But Mamma, you got a good husband in my father. Not every girl is as lucky as you. Can't you see our neighbour, Sameer Uncle? He drinks, beats his wife and yells at her every day. What is the point of getting married in the first place and cursing yourself all your life after that?"

Sensing fear in Shalini's voice, her mother asked her whether she was scared of marriage, or if she was scared of men.

"Mamma, you remember Ritu?" Shalini asked, but her mother interrupted, "Yes, I remember your friend Ritu and that she is a divorcee. She was tortured both mentally and physically for dowry by her husband and his family. Is that the reason you don't want to get married?" Her mother was trying to judge Shalini's state of mind. Shalini did not reply as she was trying to analyse her own emotions.

Her mother gave her an example of another one of her friends, Pallavi, who was happily married.

"Yes Mamma, Pallavi is happy, but hers was a love marriage."

Hearing this, her mother stood up and told Shalini to understand that in an arranged marriage, one had to trust one's parents' choice and when it came to a loved one, one needed to trust one's own instinct. However, any one of these could work or could go wrong. In the end, for a marriage to work, both the partners had to work towards the same goals. She also assured Shalini that in case she had somebody in her life, she could tell them and give them a chance to judge that person. Alternatively, she could trust them to look for a decent match for her. Shalini was about to say something when her mother told her not to answer right away and to think about it for a few days. However, that day, there was no rest for her soul. Her mother switched off the lights and went out. The next day, Shalini went to the office in a sombre mood. She did not go out of her room even during lunch time. In her free time, she studied PA and made her own notes.

It was the 25th of August. The intercom rang and Shalini's SO called out, "Your call, Shalini!" On her way to take the call, she wondered who it could be.

"Hello, is this Shalini Ma'am?" a male voice asked. She wondered who was calling her 'ma'am'. When she confirmed her identity, the voice from the other side continued,

"I am Pankaj calling from the Hindi Cell. Just wanted to confirm your presence at the vaak pratiyogita tomorrow".

It suddenly struck her that she had forgotten all about it. She thought for a moment and said, "Sir, I don't think I will be able to make it to the competition tomorrow."

While saying this, she was simultaneously trying to figure out the reason for her denial, if he asked her. And there it was. "Ma'am, can I know the reason for your backing out and please don't call me 'sir.' I am junior to you."

With her head down, she whispered that she had some important work in the office and that her SO would not allow her to participate. As soon as she looked up after keeping the receiver, her SO quizzed her smilingly, "What is it Shalini? Why do you want to malign my image?"

"Actually Sir, I have not prepared anything, nor do I intend to take part. I would rather concentrate on my work," she said and without waiting for a response, went back to her seat. She was surprised to see how her SO, whom they had nicknamed 'The silent Gazer', was not only a good observer, but for the first time had spoken a complete sentence too.

The next day she got another call on the intercom. It was Pankaj again.

"Pankaj ji, I had told you, I will not be participating. My SO will not allow me." This time she was confident and fearless.

"I understand, Ma'am, but try to understand my problem. Most of the others who had given their names have suddenly either gone on a leave today, or have refused to participate. We cannot go for the competition with only nine participants. Most importantly, I have solved your problem. My SO has already spoken to your SO, who has confirmed your presence."

"But Pankaj ji, I have not prepared anything."

She tried to express her anger through her tone on the phone and through her eyes at the SO. But Pankaj did not give up. He assured her that though she was in the second slot, he would put her in the fourth slot, so that she would have more time.

"The competition will begin at eleven and you have only thirty minutes to prepare," he said and put the phone down. Shalini looked at her SO questioningly.

The SO tried to clarify in a tone that made him sound like a thief caught red-handed. He explained that the SO of the Hindi Cell had requested that it was everyone's responsibility to promote the national language. Her SO assured Shalini all cooperation from the section and said that she should treat this like a part of her job as well. "I know you will excel in this too."

She argued that she had not prepared anything so far. If she failed to deliver on stage, would that not tarnish the image of the entire section? The SO assured her that, on the contrary, it would show their fighting spirit.

Shalini went back to her seat, thinking if no one was ready to understand, she had to start preparing without wasting any more time. She took the circular out from her drawer and chose one of the two topics given. After some time, she was ready with her first draft. With the help of a fellow assistant, Mr Das, she rehearsed; at around 11.20 she was ready to go. She closed her eyes and thought about Surbhi Aggarwal, (who had been the best Hindi debater in her school) and rehearsed twice. Everyone from her section wished her the best.

She had just taken a seat in the auditorium when her name was announced. She went with the paper in her hand and kept it on the podium. The three judges, who were joint directors, objected and told her that points would be deducted for this. She asked if she could be the last performer. Her request was granted. She went back to her section, took a corner seat facing the wall and started practicing. Nobody knew why she had come back, but no one wanted to disturb her either.

That's when Kartik came looking for her. He asked Mr Das why she was not in the auditorium for the vaak pratiyogita. Mr Das was also clueless. He told Kartik that she had just come back for reasons he didn't know and that he was going out to find out what they were. Hearing this, Kartik went back to his room thinking that she might not be participating.

After a while, Shalini got up and went straight to the auditorium where her name was announced after the non-Hindi category candidates. She faced everybody with confidence and with no trace of nervousness. Hearing the intensity of the applause, she knew her performance had been appreciated.

Since she was the last candidate, soon after, the director, who was also the chief guest, got up to give a small speech in which he referred to Shalini's debate as full of vigour, new ideas and energy. He added that more such participation was required from the younger lot so as to increase the usage of Hindi in government departments. The results were announced after that and Shalini got the second prize. As it is scientifically proven that sound travels very fast, especially through air, soon the news of her having bagged the prize also reached her section before her through the same medium.

Everyone congratulated her and told her that if she had won the second prize with an hour of preparation, she could have done wonders if she had prepared well.

Her SO appreciated her effort and told her that she owed them a party. Kartik also received the news and came to congratulate her. He was seeing her after a gap of around ten days and that seemed like a long period to him. She seemed to be in such a chirpy mood, that for the first time he told himself, "I like her. I really like her."

Her kumkum tika was shining brightly; her dupatta flying in the air due to a pedestal fan kept behind her; her big, beautiful eyes with full, arched eyebrows were something he had just noticed. He took a chair near her.

Before he could congratulate Shalini, she asked him why he had not come to see the competition. He explained how he had come when she was practicing but thought that she was not going to participate. "But I have been told that you performed really well. Even the director was all praises for you."

The people from her section called for a small impromptu party to celebrate her achievement. Kartik thought it best to leave. He congratulated her once again and left. He came back to his section and though he tried his level best to keep away from her, to not think about her, the outcome was exactly the opposite. It has been rightly said that distance makes hearts grow fonder.

That day, Shalini went home and told everyone about the vaak pratiyogita excitedly. Her mother made pakoras and tea and said that there was a surprise for her. As soon as Shalini came out of her room, she saw Raavi standing in front of her. Raavi had been her best friend since they had been in school and she now worked in Bangalore as a network engineer at Tata Infosys. Shalini was clearly surprised. The two friends hugged each other.

"What brings you here, Raavi? You never told me that you would be coming to Delhi." Shalini was excited and before Raavi could say a word, Shalini saw a wedding card in her friend's hand. Shalini asked if it was some kind of prank again.

Shalini and Raavi used to play pranks on each other. They would gift the cheapest possible gifts to each other like a used card to wish each other on the occasions of Diwali, Holi, and New Year.

Raavi handed the card to her and confirmed that it was not a prank this time. Shalini opened the card without reading the envelope and her eyes grew wide in excitement. "Good Lord! So you are getting married to Mohak finally. How did you manage to convince your parents, Raavi?"

Raavi, meanwhile, had made herself comfortable on Shalini's bed as Shalini's mother appeared with a plate of pakoras.

"Thanks, Auntyji, for keeping the secret," Raavi chuckled as she reached out for the pakoras.

"Mamma you knew that Raavi was coming? So that was the surprise! Now I will give you a surprise; Raavi is getting married." Shalini was elated and handed the card to her mother.

Raavi told Shalini's mother that everyone had to come for the wedding.

"Of course, you don't need to say that, Raavi." Shalini's mother congratulated Raavi. When she left the room, Shalini coaxed Raavi to begin the story.

"Well Shalini, the fact is that I am already married to Mohak." Raavi hesitated while sharing her little secret. Shalini froze. She just could not say anything. Raavi said, "Over," but Shalini still kept quiet.

"Oh, come on now, Shalini, we are not playing statue over here." Raavi hit her with a pillow.

"I am not surprised, I am shocked, Raavi. Do your parents know about it? How can you cheat them? How can a man, whom you have known only for the past one year become more important to you than your parents?" Shalini just did not give Raavi any chance to explain and was quite opinionated about the matter.

When Shalini finally stopped, Raavi explained that they had opted for a court marriage. Shalini was about to start off with her opinions again when Raavi simply told her to let her finish first.

She said that although her parents had approved of Mohak, his parents had not agreed as they belonged to different castes. It was then that the couple had to decide on a court marriage. Although Raavi's parents had not quite liked the idea of a court marriage and had not been a part of it, they allowed Raavi's younger brother Manav to be one of the witnesses. When Mohak had broken the news of the marriage to his parents, they had finally bowed to his decision and accepted Raavi.

"So, I have not cheated my parents and now both set of parents have met and decided on an elaborate ceremony on the 13th of November."

Shalini was listening intently.

"Tell me Shalini, what are you thinking?"

"Nothing, I was only listening to you." However, Raavi was eagerly waiting for her comments.

"I was wondering how can you trust him so much that you went for a court marriage without your parents? Don't get me wrong, if you have chosen him for yourself, he must definitely be a good guy. But, what if he cheats on you, uses you and..."

She was cut short by Raavi. "Stop, stop, please stop. Don't put so much stress on your imagination. He is a nice guy. We have been together for a year now and I know that he cannot cheat on me. My parents have given me enough wisdom to judge a person. Further, in an arranged marriage too, you or your parents judge the other person and then trust takes over. So finally, it is the trust that counts. The way I trust Mohak, even Mohak trusts me. Lastly, all marriages do not go wrong. Ninety percent of them work."

"Do both of you live together? I mean now that you are married?" Shalini asked without looking at her.

Raavi laughed out loud and said, "In Delhi, no. And in Bangalore, I won't answer and will leave it to your imagination." This time both of them laughed their hearts out. Shalini congratulated her and both of them enjoyed the evening together.

It was the 27th of August 2002. The training section had issued circulars to all the newly recruited assistants in the ministry. After reading the circular, Shalini immediately got up and went to meet Sunaina.

"Sunaina ji, what is the way out of it?" she asked hastily.

"Out of what, Shalini? Why are you so tense?" Sunaina responded, worried.

Shalini placed the circular on her table. She informed Sunaina that she was not interested in training, as she was the only woman in the group of ten trainees nominated from their ministry. Sunaina counselled her against having such a negative approach and explained that a batch in ISTM comprised participants from various ministries, so there could be a female assistant from another ministry.

She was about to leave when Sunaina asked Shalini to look at her. Shalini looked back.

"Shalini, even I was also the only woman in my batch, but I never hesitated in joining the group. The reason behind such imbalances is poor education facilities for girls, leading to thin strength of women in government jobs in our country. Do not be afraid of these boys. They are all well brought-up and well-read people. Be confident."

"Okay," is all Shalini could say and she left. She finished her work and called up ISTM to gather information about their batch. During lunch, she went to meet Kartik in the library.

"I knew I would certainly find you here at this hour of the day." Kartik looked up from his newspaper and suddenly felt a rush of blood inside him. He controlled his emotions and greeted her.

Shalini showed him the ISTM circular. Kartik knew about it. They came out of the library.

"It is very good indeed that we are getting this opportunity so early in our career, that too, within the first few months of joining. People get chances only after a year or, in some cases, even later than that. I've heard that in a few cases, the SOs or Under Secretaries do not relieve the candidates and they are not confirmed in service on time," Kartik informed her.

"Will our two year probation period be stretched if we do not complete this training within the first two years of joining?"

Kartik nodded and explained that at the end of the training, one had to pass an examination. Only two such batches were formed by ISTM in a year, "So, it is in our interest that we complete this training at the first opportunity."

"But I was...." Shalini paused. Kartik could make out from her expression that she wasn't too keen to attend the training. She added hesitantly that being the only female participant not only in their ministry, but in the entire ISTM batch, was the reason behind her dilemma.

"But, I thought you were an extrovert and a bold person," he said. Although he had not been rude, she nonetheless raised her eyebrows and asked him what he meant.

Kartik understood and tried to persuade her that he didn't mean to sound rude. What he had meant was that since she had been born and brought up in a metro, it was uncharacteristic that she'd shy away from such situations, and it was expected that she'd face them directly and boldly.

"In fact, I look up to you for your courage. Also, we'll be there to help you out in case there is a problem."

Shalini argued that there was going to be a study tour as well. It was one of the components of this training during which the batch would be taken somewhere outside Delhi. It would be difficult managing things then.

"Are you not the only woman in your section right now? Are you facing any difficulties?" Kartik's questions made Shalini rethink the matter.

Kartik wanted her to come for the training as it would be the right move for her career. Personally, he thought he would be able to get to know her better as he would get to spend a lot of time with her. Still he would need to be cautious with regard to her safety.

Shalini, on the other hand, realized that the training would be good for her. Nonetheless, she decided to inform her parents about the whole thing. Contrary to her expectations, her father was quite happy to know that Shalini was getting a chance to attend ISTM as it was the most prestigious training institute for government servants.

"You will love the environment there. Go and complete your training with a good rank as it would be an integral part of your Annual Confidential Report; it will undoubtedly make both of us proud."

Her mother added, "Just don't worry about being the only girl as you have not been raised in a conservative environment and know how to tell the difference between what is right and what is wrong."

Shalini decided that she would definitely attend the training programme.

◆

On the 31ˢᵗ of August 2002, Shalini reported to the Institute of Secretariat Training and Management, ISTM, located on the old Jawaharlal Nehru University Campus, for her Assistant Direct Recruit or ADR Training – a three-and-a-half month training module. They had lectures (by experts) on various subjects like working of the government machinery, various rules and regulations like leave rules, pension rules, conduct rules, communication, gender sensitisation, and other such subjects.

It was a two-seater bench set up. Shalini sat on the front left corner bench. As the number of seats was more than the number of participants, she sat alone. Kartik took the seat on the adjacent bench. Their course coordinator was Mr K. Swaminarain, fondly known as Swami Sir.

There were assistants from most of the ministries and departments. All of them introduced themselves and their work profiles. There were assistants from the Ministry of Railways, the Central Secretariat Services (CSS), the Armed Forces Head Quarters (AFHQ), the Ministry of External Affairs (MEA) and the Union Public Services Commission (UPSC). Their course coordinator told them that they were to choose a class representative or CR from amongst themselves.

The first thing that they were told was that they should never undermine their posts. They had been appointed as assistants to the Government of India and were considered to be the backbone of the organization. All the notings, viz., the internal discussions between the officers on a subject or case finally culminated in policy decisions are initiated at the level of an assistant.

Kartik decided that this was his chance to exploit his leadership qualities – to stop being shy, to get rid of stage fright in the longer run, and last but not the least, to impress Shalini. He told the participants from his ministry, "One of us should be the CR."

Shalini understood the importance of having the CR from among themselves, as it would help them to take decisions in their favour. She suddenly stood up and announced to her group that her vote was for Kartik. The others whole-heartedly supported this. Kartik was overwhelmed. He had got what he wanted, but he had never imagined that Shalini would be his first supporter. Later that day, he was unanimously chosen as the CR of the ADR Batch 282.

ISTM had a college atmosphere. Apart from their ADR batch, many other batches were simultaneously trained on the campus, like specialized batches on Vigilance and Disciplinary cases, Pension Benefits, other refresher courses for section officers, deputy directors, directors and so on.

They learnt that all the lecturers were from different ministries on deputation. They were made aware of the concept of deputation, which is the temporary transfer of a government employee from one government organization to another for a specified period of three or five years in public interest.

Shalini's life was peaceful as she was getting enough time to study at ISTM as well as at home. But, do good things last forever?

It was the afternoon of the 20th of October 2002 when Shalini found something scratched on her Scooty parked in the ISTM parking lot. She got a shock when she read 'Love you' scribbled on it. She looked around to check if there was anybody who she could hold responsible, but could find no one. She wondered who she could complain to about this. She saw Kartik and called out to him and told him to read what was written on her Scooty. As soon as he read it, his face became red with anger.

He asked Shalini, "Who did this?"

"Had I known, I would not have shown it to you but to Swami Sir directly."

She trusted Mr Swaminarain like a father figure; he took great care of her as she was the only girl in the batch.

Kartik told her to wait and decided to inform Mr Swaminarain. Without waiting for a response from Shalini, he turned to go upstairs to the lecturer's corridor, when he suddenly looked back and saw Shalini's tense face. He felt like hugging and consoling her. He went back and told her not to be afraid. Suddenly he saw Shyamal coming in their direction. Kartik called out to him and told him everything. He cautioned him against spreading the news any further, as it was possible the culprit was from the batch. He then requested Shyamal to stay there and went to meet Mr Swaminarain.

Shyamal patted Shalini's shoulder and said, "I am sure you are a strong girl. Don't be bothered by such stupid things or idiotic people."

Mr Swaminarain came down with Kartik, had a look at the Scooty and tried to console Shalini. However, Shalini said she was determined to find the culprit. Swami Sir said that even he was determined to punish the guy in whatever way he could.

That day, Shalini sat on the last bench for the rest of the lectures as she wasn't able to concentrate on her studies; instead she concentrated on trying to figure out who it could be. She looked at everyone carefully. Could it be Vikas from her own ministry who had tried to flirt with her? Or could it be Aman from Railways who used to tell her witty jokes, maybe to try to impress her. Who could it have been? Or was it somebody who was not from the class? That South Indian contractor who could always be seen roaming around and was supposed to be available for AC complaints or repairs?

The next day, she was cautious. She went out to Ber Sarai Market during lunch to have coffee with her group. Only Shyamal knew that Kartik lived nearby. When they came back to the ISTM campus, Shalini requested Kartik to come with her to check if somebody still loved her Scooty or if he had come to his senses by then. Kartik looked at her and both of them appreciated the joke. They checked the Scooty and found it was safe. They went back to their classroom. Their seats were kind of permanent now. She sat in her seat and suddenly stood up.

"What happened?" asked Kartik.

"Somebody loves my table too. You know, I feel this man is very gutsy, because you need guts to do this inside the classroom," she whispered indicating the words scribbled on her table.

She looked at everybody in the classroom, and suddenly had a strong feeling that the man was not from the class as no one in the batch would write on her table for the fear of getting caught.

"It is definitely an outsider trying to mislead us," she mumbled. A thought struck her and she immediately went out and found the South Indian fellow sitting outside near the water tank, staring at her. Kartik reached the spot and the other fellow left hurriedly. Shalini told Kartik that it was probably him, but she did not have proof to substantiate her claim.

"Why do you think so? He was just sitting here and not doing anything."

"I think all girls have a sixth sense and that is what makes me believe it was him."

However, Kartik insisted that they be sure before blaming anybody. During one of the breaks, Kartik insisted on knowing why Shalini suspected the technician. Shalini explained that it was just the way he looked at her while passing by, and although he was a technician for electrical appliances in the entire building, he could always be seen installed outside their room. Kartik was still not very convinced, but he supported her and said that then they would have to try to catch him red-handed.

Shalini returned home completely exhausted. Little did she know that her mother had prepared herself for the big question that day. After dinner, her mother asked her the date of Raavi's marriage.

"The 13th of November."

Her mother asked her if she had decided what she was going to gift her.

"Mummy, I have not decided anything. I want to give her something really nice, but what it is going to be is a big question and will be decided in consultation with her," Shalini explained.

"What about the big question of your life?" her mother said coming straight to the point. Shalini chose to stay quiet. Her mother knew that if Shalini decided not to say anything then she would not be able to change her daughter's mind, yet she had decided not to give up.

Her mother continued, "You will definitely gift something to Raavi. If she tells you what she needs, you will try to gift her just that. But, if she does not, then you will try to gift the best possible thing that you can. Isn't it? Similarly, marriage has to happen. If you tell us what kind of a match you want, we will try to look for such a person, but if you don't, then we will try to get the best possible match for you. So it is in your interest that you try to jot down your preferences and whatever qualities you want in your husband."

Shalini was not in a mood to discuss the topic that day so she thought of distraction.

"That means the way I might gift, let me say, a pair of earrings to Raavi, you could gift a husband to me. So, mathematically, a pair of earrings is equal to a husband."

"No, a husband is a soul-mate, a confidante, a best friend with whom you can just be yourself. A person whom you can trust more than you trust yourself." Her mother paused to see her daughter's reaction. However, when Shalini did not react, she knew that Shalini was listening carefully with her head on her mother's lap.

Her mother continued and told her how these days girls look for endless qualities in their spouse-to-be. There is nothing wrong in that, but one should always remember that even the other person might be looking for certain qualities in his bride-to-be. So one should be prepared to adjust when it comes to some of these attributes.

"Mamma, what according to you is the most important quality that cannot be compromised on?" Shalini asked.

"To me, it is loyalty and honesty," her mother answered smilingly, knowing that Shalini has grasped every word.

The next day when Shalini reached ISTM, Kartik and Shyamal took her aside and told her the plan to catch the culprit red-handed. On their request, Swami Sir had got two mobiles, one of which would be given to her. At break time, she would stay in the classroom while everyone else left. If the culprit came inside the room, she would have to press the '1' key and both Kartik and Shyamal would come and catch him.

Shalini laughed and said she felt she was a part of some spy movie. On seeing her reaction, Kartik said, "I thought you would get worried on being left alone in the room, but surprisingly, you seem to be at ease."

"On the contrary, I am actually enjoying this. When one has friends like you, then there is no need to worry," replied Shalini. Kartik smiled and Shyamal teased him secretly.

During the break that day, everyone left the room as usual. As planned, Shalini did not go out that day but stayed glued to her seat. She heard somebody opening the door and immediately touched the mobile to confirm if it was there while looking at the door. It was him, the South Indian fellow. He came inside on the pretext of checking the AC.

Shalini did not say anything and just looked at him silently. Even he did not say anything and pretended to check the AC stabilizer.

After a while, Shalini decided to initiate conversation. "What are you looking for?"

He pretended to be surprised by her presence.

"Oh! Ma'am, you are here today. I thought all of you go out during lunch."

She explained that she had decided to stay back as she had some pending work. He came near her and sat on Kartik's seat, "I have come to see if the AC is working properly."

"But, we don't use AC in the classroom."

He said, "Okay," and got up to leave.

He looked back while going out, "It was nice talking to you, Ma'am."

After this, Shalini pressed 1 on the mobile, and Kartik and Shyamal came running into the classroom. They found her sitting alone. "What happened, I had seen the fellow entering the room and had actually wanted to barge inside immediately, but Shyamal stopped me and said that we should wait for your call. Why did you not call the moment he entered the room?"

"Nothing happened," she assured them and narrated the conversation that had taken place.

"Now what?" Kartik asked.

"I think we need to give him time, because earlier I had my doubts, but now I am pretty sure that he is the one. He is probably testing the waters right now and may take two to three days to come out," she said like a pro.

"It seems you have a lot of experience at nabbing such people," said Shyamal.

"No, I watch CID a lot," Shalini retorted, making all of them laugh.

◆

The next day, the fellow came again while Shalini was inside during lunch time. He greeted her and sat next to her again. She tried to appear busy. This went on for the next two days. On the fourth day, Shalini got tired sitting inside the room and was about to go out when he appeared and said, "Hello Shalini."

"How do you know my name?"

"I heard your classmates calling you in the corridor".

"Okay! So, what have you come to check today? I told you that we don't use the AC," she said trying to make him confess.

"Like that only, Shalini, just thought to..." he hesitated.

"Thought what?"

"Nothing, was just checking if you still had pending work."

He appeared to be more confident.

"No, I had finished off my work, and I was just thinking of going out. However, it's so nice of you to show your concern," she answered, hoping that this might work.

"In fact, I am more than concerned for you Shalini".

"Means?"

"Means, can we have a coffee together?"

"Sorry, but I don't want to have anything right now."

"Can we talk? I wanted to tell you something."

"Yes, tell me."

However, before he could say anything, one of Shalini's batch-mates came in, making the technician stand up and leave hurriedly.

This time, Shalini, at Kartik's behest, had kept her mobile on, so that the two men could hear the entire conversation. As soon as he went out, they rushed to their classroom. When they entered the corridor, they observed that the South Indian fellow was sitting in his favourite seat outside the room near the water jug. Pretending he wanted water, Kartik went near him and saw him scribbling on the table.

Kartik guessed what it might be so he waited for him to complete the scribbling and drank some water in the meantime. Once he had finished, Kartik asked him what it was.

"Nothing, just like that."

The technician stood up, nervous as hell.

Kartik went to the other side of the table, and grabbed him by the collar. "What the hell do you think you were doing?"

"Nothing, Sir. Please leave me."

Kartik told Shyamal to call Swami Sir immediately. In the meantime, Shalini, hearing their voices, also came out.

Swami Sir almost ran there and read out, "Shalini I love you." He was exasperated to see that this time the man had the guts to write her name. He instructed the culprit to come to his room immediately. The culprit left with Sir, while the others revelled in their victory.

It was the morning of the 26th of October 2002. Kartik had reached ISTM and was waiting for Shalini in the parking lot. Very few owned a vehicle at that time. Swami Sir happened to pass by and asked Kartik why he was standing there. "Just like that, Sir," said Kartik.

"But, as far as I know, you do not smoke. Generally, faculty members or students who feel the urge to smoke come here. And you do not even own a vehicle... so I wonder what you are up to," Swami Sir tried to pull Kartik's leg. Kartik hesitantly said that he was waiting for Shyamal.

"Okay," said Swami Sir and suddenly saw Shalini on her Scooty. He turned back and said smilingly, "Kartik, let me tell you, Shyamal is inside the classroom."

Kartik smiled back sheepishly and waited for Sir to leave. By this time, Shalini had parked her Scooty.

"Hello CR," she greeted with her usual morning energy. Kartik greeted her too and said that he wanted to give her some good news.

"Yes, tell me what is it? But, before that, I want to order some tea in the canteen. I am feeling so cold."

While sipping hot tea in the small canteen on the campus, he informed her that the technician had been sent away from the campus.

"Oh! That's great news. Good for me and probably bad for him as he might lose his job now. But, I must tell you Kartik, not many people take up such issues empathetically. You were a great support. Had it not been for you, Shyamal and Swami Sir, I don't think we would have been able to get rid of him so easily. I thank you from the bottom of my heart."

"Shalini, I am the CR of the class. It was my duty. Also, even if I had not been the CR or if it was somebody other than you, I would still have taken up the issue with the same sensitivity," he replied and felt like a hero.

As both of them left for class, Shalini decided that Kartik was basically a good human being and Kartik thought, "I am definitely on her friends' list now." They entered the class together. Swami Sir was already inside.

He said, "Shyamal, Kartik was waiting for you in the parking lot. He has some important news for you."

Everybody looked at Kartik. Shalini took her seat. Kartik went straight to Sir in the centre of the classroom and looked at Sir as if trying to request him to stop pulling his leg. Swami Sir was intelligent enough to understand. He said, "Yes Kartik, tell them about our study tour."

Kartik took the hint and informed everyone that the tour dates had been finalized from the 8th of November to the 20th of November 2002. He then explained the procedure.

"We have to decide which part of the country we want to visit and tell the management our decision by tomorrow. The trip will be managed by us. All of us will collectively decide and delegate responsibilities for keeping accounts, booking tickets, food and transportation for local tours and lodging. Sir will help us by giving us the details of the lodging and transport arrangements that the previous batches had done. All of us will get the second half of the day off tomorrow to get the money sanctioned from our offices, which we need to deposit in ISTM. Guys, the trip should be informative as well as fun, so we should choose the place accordingly," he concluded.

That day during lunch, no one went out. There was total chaos. No one wanted to visit their home state as they thought that there would be nothing new to see. Kartik and group decided that they wanted to visit the southern part of the country. After reaching a consensus, Kartik went to the class dais and requested everyone's attention. He asked if at least ministry-wise they had reached a conclusion.

"No," everyone replied unanimously.

Kartik continued that he knew no one wanted to visit their home towns, more so because the government had offered the facility of home town LTC for that. He added that their group has thought of an ideal location that had no representation in class.

"South India."

"Chennai is a good bet. Sir also confirmed we can cover some nearby places too," said Virender from the Railways Ministry.

Kartik was prepared for this. He informed him, "We will have two industrial visits, one each in Chennai and Ooty. Our journey will commence from Rameswaram, a holy place. We can also visit some of the beaches in Chennai and close to Madurai for some fun. Another thing is that Swami Sir belongs to the area, so he can add some more places to our itinerary."

Everybody listened carefully and gave the proposal a thumbs up.

Shalini wondered why did Kartik suffer from stage fright when he had such good leadership qualities. She was sure that he could be a very good speaker.

She reached home and told her parents about the study tour. It was when she was telling them the dates that she suddenly realized that it coincided with Raavi's wedding which she could not miss. She decided to back out of the tour.

Her father asked if the tour was going to earn her some marks.

"Ten marks. But Papa, how can I not attend Raavi's wedding?" she asked.

"I am not telling you to miss the tour, nor am I telling you to miss the wedding. It is entirely your call; keep in mind that neither of these opportunities will come again in life," her father stated.

Shalini decided that she would go to the wedding. The next day, she went straight to Kartik, who was busy delegating tour duties to everyone.

Shalini greeted everybody. Kartik informed her that booking the tickets from the counter was her duty since the ladies' line was a shorter one. She mustered the courage to say that although she would book the tickets, she would not be able to go on the study tour.

"What do you mean you are not coming? No one can back out. You have to attend the tour as there are marks for it." Kartik was furious.

"But, I have a problem. I cannot go on these dates."

Kartik thought that 'these dates' meant that she would perhaps be getting her periods then.

Is that a reason to back out of the tour? he thought to himself.

He was trying to ascertain the reason when he saw that Shalini was about to speak again. Kartik immediately requested her to wait for a while till he finished allocating duties. Later, he came out of the classroom with Shalini and asked her to tell him exactly what the problem was. She explained her reasons. Kartik thought he had been very stupid to think of a reason which she would never have stated even if that had been the case.

He saw her tense face and said, "It is a very unintelligent reason for not going for the tour. Friends are important, but your career is important too. I feel Swami Sir will not allow this."

"Will you come along with me to meet Swami Sir?" she asked. Kartik agreed, though unwillingly. On their way to Swami Sir's room, he was thinking, and in fact praying, that Sir would not agree to her request. He had been looking forward to the trip. It was a chance to get to know her even better.

They reached Sir's room and suddenly heard loud noises coming from inside it. It appeared that Sir was furious at one of their classmates Vinayak for wanting to back out of the tour. They went a little closer, pressed their ears to the door and heard Sir say that not even the Director would allow it.

"This study tour is an integral component of the entire training and even if the reason is your brother's wedding, you cannot opt out of it. You only have two options: either come along or be deported back to your ministry where you will be made to give a written explanation and attend the training all over again."

Kartik and Shalini backed off when they heard footsteps coming towards the door. Vinayak had come out and was very tense. Kartik took Shalini aside and asked her if she still wanted to try her luck. Shalini shook her head and both of them returned to the classroom. Kartik was happy and Shalini was worried. She realized that she would not be able to attend Raavi's marriage.

During break time, he suggested, "Shalini, why don't you explain to your friend your reasons for not being able to be a part of the celebrations." She nodded and called up Raavi to explain everything.

To Shalini's surprise, her friend took it quite sportingly, "No problems dear. I will look forward to your visit once you are back. And one more thing, I want to see you hitched to a good guy soon and I will definitely attend your wedding."

Shalini smiled and wondered if she really knew somebody good enough to get hitched to. "God, what am I thinking? I should concentrate on the CSE," she said and tried to calm her racing mind.

"You need to buy a stroller to pack your things for the tour. You can go to Sarojini Nagar market from your Institute during lunch tommorrow," Shalini's mother suggested that night, so as to get the tour preparations rolling.

Shalini decided that she would miss a part of her lecture before lunch and leave at about 12.30 p.m. So the next day, at about noon, Swami Sir called Kartik to the administration block for some urgent work related to the tour. The lecturer objected saying that he was teaching a very important topic and excusing even one of the students would not be in their interest. He, however, assured Swami Sir that the class would be free by 12.45 p.m. Swami Sir agreed.

Shalini understood that requesting Sir to let her to go out to buy the stroller would be useless at this point. She waited for the class to get over and decided that she would request Kartik to accompany her to the market on her Scooty so that she could be back on time. Kartik, however, left to meet Swami Sir when the class got over. Shalini was in a dilemma. Suddenly, she saw Shyamal and requested him to come with her. Shyamal agreed. They returned at 2.30 p.m. They had missed thirty minutes of Swami Sir's session. They took their seats, but the seat next to Shalini was empty.

Where has Kartik gone? Shalini wondered. He never sits anywhere else. Swami Sir had called him for some work but Sir is here in class. Where is Kartik? She was lost in her own world when suddenly Swami Sir asked her a question. Since she had been lost in her thoughts, she kept quiet. She apologized for not having listened.

It is said that you cannot hide anything from your mother, lawyer and doctor. However, it is difficult to hide things from your teacher as well. Sir knew what the others didn't know yet.

He said unabashedly, "What is happening here? You were not listening and Kartik has a headache and is sitting at the back with his head down. Come on, you two were amongst the brightest students of the batch. Do not behave in a childish manner."

Shalini immediately turned at the mention of Kartik's name. He was there, his head still down. Sir smiled and even Kartik could not help but feel embarrassed. Shalini understood that her actions had actually given gossipmongers fodder. She did not look up from her book for the rest of the class.

After the class she went up to Kartik to ask if he wanted to have a cup of tea or coffee, but Kartik got up and went out to wash his face. Shyamal went after him too.

"What is the matter with you?" Kartik did not reply and was about to come out of the washroom, when Shyamal pulled him back and explained how Shalini had requested him to come buy a suitcase with her.

"As you were not around, I thought I needed to help her out. What's the problem in that?"

Kartik, however, said, "There is no need to explain anything. I just have a headache and will be fine soon."

He thought that Shalini came to him for every small little thing, then why had she approached Shyamal for this? He went back to the classroom and sat at the back. Shalini asked him if he was fine. He nodded. She requested him to come back to his seat but he refused politely.

That day, she did not approach him again, nor did he come around. However, while driving back home, she was thinking about it. When she reached home, she quickly changed her clothes and sat with her books in front of her, but she couldn't concentrate as she wondered why she was feeling so affected.

"I need to clear the Civil Services exam. I am ambitious. Kartik is good, but I should not think about him. Please stop, stop, stop!"

She opened her books and tried hard to concentrate.

Kartik was struggling with his emotions as well. That night he wondered why he was not taking it easy as they were only friends. Why was he feeling jealous when he was not even sure of his own feelings? Moreover, Shyamal is married and I trust him. Had I been there, Shalini probably would have requested me to go with her, he thought.

These thoughts were bothering him, not letting him sleep. Nonetheless, he was determined that he would behave normally with her the next day.

The following day, Shalini had decided to keep her distance from Kartik who was already at his seat. When he saw Shalini, he wished her. She wished him too and both got down to their books. Since Shalini had not brought up the previous day's issue with Kartik, he started feeling guilty about his behaviour.

He initiated a conversation. He let her know that they would be going to book the tickets the following day in Rajan's van if it was okay with her. She nodded and the conversation ended as Kumar Sir entered the room.

Kartik lost attention in the lecture as his interest was outweighed by his guilt for the previous day's behaviour. He thought of an idea to begin another conversation.

He wrote in his diary, "How much did the bag cost you?" and passed it to Shalini.

She wrote, "Why do you want to know?" and passed it back.

"I am sorry about yesterday's behaviour. The truth is I was just not myself."

"Okay, but why?" Shalini passed the diary back, but immediately thought, "Why am I eager to know that? I should probably not have written that."

Kartik was mature enough to understand and knew the answer could bring an end to their friendship too.

So he wrote back, "I was not feeling well yesterday. Now can you tell me how much it cost you?"

"Nine hundred rupees. And now, please let me study."

The next morning, they went to book the tickets. Suddenly Rajan, one of the senior most participants, who was in the driver's seat, observed that Kartik had been wearing the same shirt for the past three days. He asked Kartik the reason for this. All eyes were on Kartik who, in turn, felt embarrassed. Since an explanation of sorts was expected of him, he said that it had been a gift from his elder brother and he liked it very much. That's when Shalini remembered that she had paid Kartik a compliment about the shirt two days ago.

I do that with all of my good friends and family members. Is my compliment the reason he has not taken off the shirt since then? No, that can't be. After all, there is something called hygiene. How can he forget about it, just because of a compliment? Uff, however hard I may try to get this emotion out of my system, it creeps in again and again, she thought.

◆

It was the afternoon of the 8th of November 2002. Everyone had to reach the Nizammuddin Railway Station to board the Nizammuddin-Chennai Rajdhani Express. Shalini reached the station with her parents and brother who had come to see her off. The station was crowded with three or four people coming to drop each passenger, as was the case with Shalini. Kartik was already in the train. He helped Shalini with her luggage. Shalini introduced Kartik and Shyamal to her family.

Kartik saw that Shalini looked exactly like her mother but had inherited her big nose from her father. Her father chatted with the boys while her mother chose to give Shalini some quick tips.

The train whistled and the journey began as Shalini bid her parents goodbye. Half the bogie was booked for the group. Shalini seated herself on the lower seat on the side. For some time after that, she chose to keep to herself. After a while, Kartik came to her seat, gauged her mood and made himself comfortable beside her. He asked if it was her first trip without her parents.

"Earlier I had gone for an NCC trip to Chennai from my school, Sadhu Vaswani International School for Girls. But there is a small difference; that was an all-girls trip and this one..."

She had not completed her sentence when he added that this one was an all boys' trip with Shalini being the only exception. Both of them laughed. After a while there was silence again.

He decided to apply the Thought Diversion Process to change her mood. But, what could that diversion be? He noticed that some of the boys had taken out playing cards. He thought maybe she would like a game of chess.

He went to ask the others if anyone had brought along a chess set. Rajan obliged. Kartik brought the game to Shalini's seat. She smiled when she saw the game. "How did you guess that I really like this game? Though, I am not very good at it!"

"Let's see, who is better," Kartik challenged her.

They played the first game for over an hour and continued. Shalini won a few while Kartik won some. But, neither of them was ready to give up. They played and discussed things ranging from chess to PA.

I have already started loving this journey. May it never end, he thought.

Suddenly they were distracted by the soup vendor.

"Oh! I love soup, and the soup served in Rajdhani train is the best," Shalini said as she took her glass and told the vendor to bring anything that he had left back to their compartment. The soup vendor nodded happily.

Shalini praised the soup so much that everyone had it very enthusiastically. Shyamal stated that he was having soup for the first time. Nagendra nodded and added that most of them had come there from remote villages that did not have even basic facilities like electricity. So how would they know what soup was? Everybody agreed. When the soup vendor came back, Shyamal instructed him to leave the container there and it took all of them hardly fifteen minutes to empty the container!

Shalini said thoughtfully that if they could crack such a tough examination despite coming from such humble backgrounds, their achievement was definitely worth celebrating and everyone raised their glasses of soup and cheered.

It was a nice day, ending with a spate of jokes. Later at night, when Shalini lay down on her berth, she thought she had chosen her berth well as she was with everyone, yet she could still be by herself.

The next day in the train, Rajan offered to play chess with both Kartik and Shalini. He would play with them one after the other. Rajan was good at the game and soon defeated both of them in separate games. Shalini proposed to team with Kartik to play against Rajan. The other two agreed. This time, the team won. Rajan commented, "You people make a good pair."

"A good team," Shalini corrected him, while Kartik secretly felt happy at Rajan's choice of words.

They reached Chennai at 11.30 p.m. on the 9th of November. Due to a technical glitch, the Rajdhani Express, which usually was on time, was late by three hours. A TTDC Bus was waiting outside the station for them. It was a deluxe 2x2 coach. Their luggage was loaded on the roof of the coach. Shalini could not make her way to the entrance to the bus as there were boys in the way, eager to get into the bus to grab their favourite seats before the others. She requested Kartik, who was closer to the entrance, to keep a window seat for her in the front.

She knew that the back seats would be occupied by the boys so that they could have their share of fun. She thought it would be prudent to sit on one of the front seats either alone or maybe with Sir.

Kartik got into the bus and sat on the third seat, while Shalini was waiting for her turn at the entrance to the bus.

Shyamal, who was already in the bus, shouted from the back calling Kartik there. Kartik, gestured for him to wait. When Shalini got into the bus, Kartik gave her the third seat.

Once comfortable at the window seat, she asked, "Where are you going to sit?"

"Do you have any problem if I sit with you?"

"I don't have any problem, in fact, I will have good company. But your friends might miss you or make fun of you."

"As the CR, it is my responsibility to take care of everyone."

"But this way, the CR is only taking care of one person, what about the others?"

"Look, a few of the boys could have brought alcohol along. So, in the interest of your safety, I pledge to be with you most of the time," Kartik took an oath jokingly. "But, even you could have brought some alcohol."

Before he could reply, Swami Sir introduced everyone to Mr Shankar, their guide for the rest of the tour. Shankar was a middle-aged fellow and seemed like a seasoned guide.

He introduced himself in a typical South Indian accent, "Good evening friends. I am Shankar, your tour guide. We were supposed to take you to Pondicherry first, but due to the delay in the arrival of the train, we have now made arrangements for a night over at Chennai TTDC Hotel. Tomorrow morning by 10.00 a.m. we will go to Rameswaram."

There was a lot of noise and chaos as the boys were still trying to settle down. Kartik got up and asked everyone to settle down fast. He went around the whole bus and helped people, had a few quick words with Sahil and Shyamal who were waiting for him and came back to Shalini.

"I was waiting for you," said Shalini.

"Why?"

"Although I can take care of myself, but if people have actually got alcohol, then the seat beside me should not remain empty."

"But as you said, even I could have got some..." he teased her. She responded confidently that if that had been the case, she would have been sitting alone, or with Sir for that matter.

"But, I trust you Kartik..."

Kartik thought that this was a good sign. She trusts me. Wow!

"...After all, you are the CR of the group," she added, completing her sentence.

Oh! That way. So, Kartik, she trusts you because you are the CR and not because you are Kartik Vats, he thought and smiled again.

Once they reached the beautiful hotel lobby, Swami Sir instructed Kartik, "Not more than two boys are to be allowed in a room and a separate room to be given to Shalini, which shouldn't be at the end of the corrridor."

Kartik quickly delegated the tasks to five other boys, one each from a ministry and instructed them accordingly. He kept a room in the middle of the corridor for Shalini and told the hotel staff to help her with her luggage. His room, which he was going to share with Shyamal, was the one adjacent to Shalini's room. It was a first-rate hotel, centrally located, with proper ventilation and a good ambience.

The next morning, they gathered again at the hotel lobby, ready to leave for Rameswaram. Their luggage was reloaded onto the bus and they all took their seats. Shalini and Kartik chose the same seats again. The nine-hour-long bus journey began at 11.00 a.m. after breakfast. They halted at around 2.00 p.m. for lunch. After lunch, most of the young recruits dozed off. There was silence in the bus. Shalini also slept with her head against the window, trying to make sure that her head did not fall on the other side onto Kartik's shoulder.

At about 5.00 p.m., the bus suddenly stopped on a highway. She waited for an announcement from Shankar, the guide. However, there was none. Most of the boys, including Sir, got off the bus.

Shalini peeped out of the window to find out the reason for this and saw the backs of some of the boys relieving themselves.

"Oh God, did I have to see that?" she murmured, feeling embarrassed.

"What happened?" asked Kartik who was still feeling sleepy.

"See for yourself."

He tried to peep out of the window and his face brushed past her shoulders. He could smell the fragrance of her body and feel the soft touch. They both looked at each other while he was still slightly bent over her. Although he was a bit sleepy, the sleepiness could not mute the pleasant feeling of her soft touch.

He immediately recovered and got off the bus with his camera. Shalini decided not to think about it or she'd go crazy and looked out of the window from the other side.

It was scenic, but she was feeling too lazy to get up and also feared that she might see one of the men relieving himself if she tried too hard to peep out of the window. She saw Kartik taking photographs on the other side.

The bus began its journey once all of them climbed back on. Once Kartik was seated, she said, "Kartik, maybe I am wrong, but couldn't we have stopped at a public restroom in a petrol pump? Imagine, what a sight these people were making for the passers-by?"

"I completely agree with you Shalini, but I don't have a say in everything."

They reached Rameswaram at about 9.30 p.m. and trooped to their rooms in the TTDC hotel. They collected in the dining hall for dinner but as all of them were tired, they retired to their rooms soon.

The next morning, on the 11th of November, they had to wake up early to offer prayers at the Rameswaram temple which was a walkable distance from the hotel. Out of the twelve, it is believed that the visit to Rameswaram is equal to visiting the rest of the eleven jyotirlingas, as the Shivalinga here is believed to have been made by Lord Rama himself.

Visitors had to make a reasonable payment to the panditji, who then made the devotees take a bath with water taken from twenty-two *kundas*, while chanting the name of their *gotra*, forefathers, etc. All the members of the group along with Sir performed the ritual. Once inside the temple, it was very peaceful; nothing but the chanting of mantras could be heard. Everyone came out at about 8.00 a.m. Sir allowed them four hours to explore places nearby, after which they were to leave for Coimbatore.

All of them quickly formed groups, took autos and went to visit the nearby areas. Shalini decided to stay back rather than go cramped with the boys in an auto. She saw that Sir was staying back and so was Aman.

Once inside her room, she quickly packed her bags for the next journey. She was unable to decide what to do next. She saw Aman outside her room's window and asked him what he was doing there.

"Nothing, was just feeling hungry so thought of soaking up vitamin S from the sun," he chuckled.

She smiled and went out to join him. "How has your trip been so far?" he asked. She paused to find the right words to answer that one; she finally summed it up in one word, "Fine."

"But, I must commend your guts for being a part of an all-boys group."

"Hmmm," she replied briefly as if not wanting to discuss it. "Why did you not go out with the rest?" she asked.

"Because I wanted to be with you," he laughed, but added, "The truth is I found the temple so serene that I wanted some time alone after that."

"Oh! Then I must be disturbing you."

"No, it's okay! It is always nice to be in good company rather than being in the company of a bunch of rowdy boys."

She felt embarrassed. "You never give up flirting, do you?"

This time he changed the topic by asking her the same question. She thought hard about it but could not find a suitable answer. Was it because the autos were crowded or was it because nobody had even asked her to accompany them? Nonetheless she answered that even she wanted to be in good company at which both had a hearty laugh.

They went to the dining area, ordered some idlis and vadas and had a good time chatting and eating. Sir joined them at 11.30 a.m., the boys returned soon after, and at noon, everyone was at the reception with their luggage.

Swami Sir told Kartik to stay back with him to pay the bills. The rest of them took their seats in the bus, which by now were kind of permanent. The second seat, that is, the seat in front of Shalini and Kartik's seat (which had remained empty so far) was now occupied by Aman. Swami Sir and Kartik climbed in and the bus started. Shankar the guide told them that very soon they were going to see the Pamban Bridge.

The novelty of this bridge was that it was a low bridge on the Pamban river with a railway track built on it, which opened up in the middle to allow smooth passage to passing ships beneath it.

Vendors were selling pieces of cucumber and pineapple on the roadways bridge which was way above the Pamban Bridge. They enjoyed the roadside food and the beauty of the place but Shalini felt it would have been wonderful had they been able to watch the bridge opening up to let the ships pass.

The batch moved on to their next destination, which was around six hours away. During the first thirty minutes of the drive, Shalini and Kartik had made no effort to speak to each other. They were busy taking pictures and seeing the sights. The journey was however too long to keep to oneself, so Shalini took the lead.

She asked what they had seen in Rameswaram.

"Oh! It was really nice. We visited Dhanushkhodi Temple, Rama Tirtham, Hanuman Temple and Jatayu Temple, but enjoyed ourselves the most at Dhanushkodi Beach," he narrated excitedly and asked her why she had not accompanied them.

"Because you never asked me to," she felt like saying but commented wryly that she just had not felt like going out.

"Since Aman had not gone out either, he kept company. We joked, took a stroll, feasted on some good South Indian delicacies together; in short, had a good time."

"Good," was all he could say, but his mind was racing (though it was his heart that was racing).

How could I forget about her? How would she have dealt with five boys in one auto? Why did I not realize this earlier? Am I supposed to worry about this now? By now, I know at least this much about Shalini that she likes good-natured, witty people and that is exactly what Aman is. God, maybe that is why he is suddenly sitting in the seat in front of us. But, I am still not sure about my thoughts. I cannot decide. But, why am I feeling insecure? What the hell? I do not know what to do.

Kartik's mind was flooded with such thoughts and questions. His train of thought was suddenly broken when at around 4.00 p.m. the bus stopped at Madurai near a restaurant for lunch.

Shyamal, one of the people in charge of finances, announced that anyone who wanted to have non-vegetarian food could have it as their budget allowed it. They made two groups and sat at two different tables – one for vegetarians and the other for non-vegetarians.

The vegetarians observed that the prices of the non-veg food were way higher than the veg food. Aman and Shalini were both vegetarians and they decided to take up the issue with Sir as they had been clearly instructed before the commencement of the tour that any additional expenditure apart from what had been sanctioned by the government, would have to be borne by the members equally. A confrontation broke out. The vegetarians demanded that they should not be made to pay anything if the total expenditure increased, while the non-vegetarians pleaded that everybody had the right to have food as per their taste.

Shyamal and Sahil were the leaders from the non-vegetarian group and Shalini led the vegetarian group. Kartik thought getting into this confrontation would not be a good idea. He pleaded with Shyamal that after this they'd all have veg food. If anyone wanted to have non-veg sometimes, they could pay for it themselves. He could not understand the fuss about not having non-veg food for ten days. Everyone agreed and patched up. Shalini was impressed with Kartik again and Kartik noticed that.

Later in the bus when Kartik saw that Shalini was in a good mood, he asked her, "Do you have any elder brothers or sisters?"

She said she did not, "But why do you want to know this?"

"Just like that."

"No, I insist on knowing why."

"Oh! Was just thinking your parents will probably be looking for a match for you".

She nodded. "But, I have requested them to wait till CSE-2003.

Both of them enjoyed the lush green belt on NH49 and did not speak to each other for a few minutes until they decided to say something at the same time. They looked at each other and had a good laugh. Finally, Kartik requested Shalini to speak first.

"What about your family and your marriage plans?"

"Now, somebody is interested in my marriage plans," he teased her.

"So, you are seeing somebody?" she teased back.

He blushed but Shalini assured him that there was no need to be tense, and that he could confide in her.

"I have four brothers and one sister. My three elder siblings are married and my family is currently looking for a match for my elder brother. Further, we are also concentrating on my younger brother's job; he is preparing for government exams."

"And what about your girlfriend?"

"Come on, Shalini. Stop it now."

"Okay, now it's your turn. You wanted to say something," she said.

He said it was nothing. There was silence between them for a while. She insisted that as it was a long journey, they'd need something to talk about.

"So please don't become silent like Amitabh Bachchan in *Sholay*. I like to see him in jovial roles like the one in *Chupke Chupke*. Please go ahead and say something."

He smiled at her innocence and said, only to pass time, he wanted to know what qualities she wanted in her life partner.

"Good question. I asked my mother the same question recently and based on her explanation, I have formed my own opinion. I want him to be a *jugaadu* number one," she said on an impulse.

"And I thought you were an Amitabh Bachchan fan, but you actually seem to be a Govinda fan... jugaadu number one," he laughed.

"A jugaadu, as we were taught during our MBA, is a good manager, one who can find a way out of any difficult situation. He is a good leader. I want him to be just that and he should be a pleasure to be with, a teetotaller and a pure vegetarian."

She seemed to be in a tell-all mood.

He was amused at such a different kind of approach towards thinking about a life partner. Generally, a girl's approach was that her partner be tall, dark, handsome, financially stable, and so on.

"Maybe, but I am different," she giggled. Kartik asked her about the vegetarian clause.

"I feel that you cannot take away anybody's life just to satiate your taste buds. That is why I was on Aman's side today."

She explained that as a Sindhi she followed the teachings of Sadhu Vaswani, in whose memory Sindhis celebrate the 25th of November, his birth anniversary, as a Meatless Day.

It was 7.00 p.m. when the bus halted again. The boys got down and by this time even Shalini had got used to their ritual. However, this time, it was a bit different. Even she wanted to relieve herself. But, whom could she confide in? Why didn't they remember that there was a lady in the group as well?

She looked outside the window and observed that it was already dark. Not even a single passer-by could be seen, though there were some small houses on the right side. Shalini was eagerly waiting for Kartik to climb back on the bus. When he did, she told him hesitantly that she had a request.

"Shoot please," he said.

She paused, but gave in and said, "Even I want to go out for the same purpose."

He wondered where he could take her as this was an unexpected situation.

"Please inform Sir to stop at some place where public conveniences are available," she requested him.

He went and spoke to Sir who was sitting in the cabin of the bus with Shankar. "Shankar guide says that there would be no restaurant or hotel on the way for the next two hours. So, if you could wait till then, its okay, or else you could come out with me, and we would look for some place." He told her, hoping at the same time that she would choose to wait. However, she stood up. He stood up too looking at her questioningly.

"What?"

"What what? I am coming out with you."

They went out on to the right side where the small houses were located. None of them was open and had no trace of life or light. They went into the lane nearby, from where they could see some light coming from the other end. It was dark otherwise.

Shalini held Kartik's hand as she was feeling scared. "Don't worry Shalini. I am with you," he said and felt like a filmi hero again. They went near the house from where the light was coming.

In unison they asked if somebody was there. Although the door was open, nobody came out, so they knocked on it. An old lady wearing a white sari, her white hair tied back, came out walking slowly. She looked at them as if they were from some other planet.

While trying to peep inside the small house Shalini said politely that they were students from Delhi on a study tour. "Just wanted to use your washroom."

However, the lady stopped her from entering inside and said something that was probably in Tamil. They could not understand a word.

Kartik stopped Shalini from opening her mouth and feeling that the old lady might not have heard properly due to her old age, said aloud, "Auntyji, bathroom please." This time, Auntyji tried to push them back.

Shalini said, "Auntyji please toilet, shauchalaya."

Auntyji said, "Ille, ille."

Kartik asked Shalini how many more synonyms she knew for the word 'washroom'.

"None that I can think of in my current position."

Shalini told Kartik to keep the lady busy so that she could go inside and do her job. Nobody else seemed to be inside the house, or else they would have definitely come out on hearing the noise.

Kartik kept the old lady busy in a one-sided conversation. Shalini slipped inside. While Shalini was trying to come out, Auntyji (having taken note of the fact that Shalini had gone inside the house) thought she was a thief. The old lady immediately took a wooden plank and was about to hit Shalini when Kartik pulled Shalini towards himself. Without losing another second, he took her hand and ran towards the bus. After a while, they looked back and saw that the auntyji, now followed by three elderly men, had got tired and seemed to have stopped following them.

They came back to the bus, pretending nothing had happened. Both of them sat in their seats and heaved a sigh of relief. Kartik was disturbed by the episode, while Shalini seemed to have enjoyed the adventure.

Kartik went inside the bus cabin again. Swamy Sir said to him, "I have now instructed Shankar that the bus will be stopped at places with public conveniences." Kartik came back and informed Shalini about it and told her that he was going to the back to meet Shyamal for a while. He knew Shyamal was still upset about the conflict over food.

"Why the hell are you helping her so much when she does not even care about us? Had she been thoughtful enough, she would have not become a part of the group fussing over as petty a matter as having non-vegetarian food!" Shyamal shouted.

Kartik gestured for Shyamal not to shout. He tried to justify his stance by saying that as the CR, it was his duty to make sure everyone was taken care of and that she was strictly against non-vegetarianism.

"Kartik, I know things which probably even you have not acknowledged so far. However, as a friend, I should caution you about one thing. Delhi girls cannot be trusted. Believe me," Shyamal whispered.

"Please cool down. We will talk later inside our room," he said and went back to sit with Shalini, who had fallen asleep with her head against the window.

As soon as he reached, he saw Aman standing near her seat. Kartik asked wryly, "Do you want to sit here?"

"Oh! I just wanted to help her as I felt that she could have fallen on the other side as she was sleepy." Before Kartik could say anything, Shalini got up. "Don't worry Aman, I can take care of myself."

The group finally reached Coimbatore at midnight.

All of them were tired and hungry as the bus had not stopped for dinner anywhere since they had been running behind schedule.

They went to their respective rooms at the TTDC Hotel in Coimbatore. A few of them simply hit their beds without dinner. However, Sir, Shyamal, Kartik, Shalini, Nagendra and a few others still managed to come out as they could not control their hunger pangs. The cafeteria in the hotel was closed, so they tried looking for restaurants outside the hotel. At one in the morning, however, one should not have too many expectations. Fortunately, they sighted a local vendor a few meters away from the hotel, selling paranthas in the South Indian style with curry leaves sprinkled on them.

Shalini was not very hungry but she simply enjoyed being awake and out at that hour. After an hour, all of them went back to their respective rooms with instructions from Sir that they would be required to get up early in the morning to leave for their next destination – Ooty.

Shalini was feeling wide awake when she returned to her room. At such times she felt lonely and craved female company. She stood beside the window for a few minutes, thinking about the journey so far and realized that Sunainaji had indeed been right when she had told Shalini that the group consisted of educated people and her worries had proven to be baseless. She had already become friends with most of them and Kartik, in particular, was a good person.

Shalini did not realise when she dozed off, only to be woken up by a call on the intercom. Kartik let her know that it was already 7.15 a.m. and that they were supposed to leave by 8.00 a.m. He told her to come down for breakfast quickly. Although she was still feeling sleepy and did not feel like going anywhere, she still replied that she would be there in twenty minutes.

Later, while having her breakfast, she was also told that Sir had taken a round and knocked on all the doors and she had been the only one who had not responded. She remembered how her mother used to try hard to wake her up when she had been in school or sometimes even during her college days. She missed her mother a lot that day.

The bus had barely started moving when Shankar the guide took the mic and informed them that they were supposed to start for Ooty at 6.00 a.m. However, due to the delay, there had been a change in the program and they would now go to Ooty via Karaikal. Karaikal was beautiful and was about six-and-a-half hours away from their current location.

The participants came up with the idea of demonstrating their hidden talents during their journey. At first, they played *Antakshari,* a game where teams were supposed to sing songs starting from the last letter of the previous song. Later, a few of them came up with jokes, songs and *hasyakavitas*, or poetry invoking laughter. Kartik came up with a poem on the topic of saving the girl child. Everyone, including Sir, appreciated Kartik's poem. Kartik, however, proved to be the last participant because after such a serious take on a social problem, everyone wanted a break.

By 11.00 a.m. most of them were so tired that they fell asleep. They halted near a restaurant three hours later, had their lunch and rushed back so they could reach Karaikal in time. In another hour, they had reached the place which was even more beautiful than the guide had described.

The beauty of the place lay in the backwaters flowing from the river Arasalar, in between the rock-mountains. The width of the area covered by the water varied. Somewhere the stretches were very narrow, allowing only one boat at a time, and elsewhere they were so huge that they could accommodate fifty boats.

They decided to go boating. There were special bowl-shaped boats and one boat could accommodate four or five people including the boatman, depending on the weight of the people.

They had to hire seven boats to accommodate everyone. Shalini, Kartik, Shyamal and Sahil decided to go in one boat.

As they began their ride, the boatman in his early fifties had no problem rowing the boat as they were going downstream. He asked them if they had watched the movie *Roja*. Everyone nodded to say they had. He revealed proudly that a part of the movie shoot had taken place there and that he had been one of the boatmen who had appeared in the movie too. Everyone applauded.

On the way back, an upstream journey, the boatman was horribly slow. The boats of their colleagues were being rowed parallel to theirs. They took pictures of each other and had fun. However, when it started growing dark at around 6.00 p.m., they realized that only their boat was in the water. The boys offered to help the boatman to row the boat.

He refused and explained that as it was upstream, untrained people would not be able to row the boat. He tried his best but after a while, gave up and just managed to row his boat close to the rocky hills. He then held on to one of the rocks tightly. They could now feel the heat of the situation and looked at the boatman for an answer. He told them not to worry as these things happened and help would come soon.

Shalini was enjoying the adventure. "What a situation to be in! We are in the middle of a river and so far there is nobody in sight to come to our rescue."

On the other hand, Sahil had already pressed the panic button, "Look, I am the only son of my parents. I got this job recently and my parents need me. Please do something."

Swami Sir had reached the shore. He realized that the only girl had not arrived, so he sent one boat back. The four in the boat were also holding the rock now and could see the boat coming back. The boatman of the new boat reached close to them and spoke to the old man in his language. When they reached a conclusion; the old boatman requested two of the passengers to shift to the other boat.

Immediately, both Sahil and Shalini spoke in unison. While Sahil said that he would not go out in the middle of the river, Shalini just didn't want to miss out on the adventure. Shyamal, who was about to open his mouth, was silenced by Kartik who decided to go with Shalini. The two boats then moved back slowly, although Shyamal's boat was still lagging behind.

Shyamal shouted, "You two selfish skinny people should have actually stayed behind in this old man's boat, allowing us to move to the new boat!" Shalini and Kartik chose to simply laugh it off. It was already dark when they reached the shore.

Swami Sir seemed worried, but regained his composure upon seeing Kartik and Shalini return. He immediately said that he had been worried for her and asked about the rest of the party. Shalini informed him about what had happened. As soon as Shyamal and Sahil reached the shore, they ran after Kartik and had a mock fight. At 7.00 p.m. all of them boarded the bus which soon sounded like a fish market as all of them were eager to share their own experiences.

Around thirty minutes later, Shankar informed them that they were now heading to Ooty. They would visit HPF – Hindustan Photo Film – a public sector undertaking and the chief industrial unit of the district along with making a visit to the Tribal Museum. "And now the most important announcement – Ooty is approximately 432 kilometres from here. It will take approximately nine hours and we will reach by 4.00 a.m. We will go directly to HPF. So guys, enjoy your night in the bus itself."

Shalini asked loudly, "Shankar Sir, which organization is open at four in the morning?"

"They work round the clock, Ma'am. That is the reason this visit is so important for you people, so that you can study their work culture," Shankar replied.

After the announcement, instead of sounding like a fish market, the bus seemed to have turned into a mourning room. After a while, the bus stopped so the students could have dinner. Shalini decided to have a very light dinner and no water lest she had to hunt for another toilet. That night was not at all comfortable. Shalini, who was always sitting in the window seat lay her shoulder against the window, but Kartik had no such luxury.

Kartik made the best use of the time he spent in the bus with Shalini. That day, Kartik asked her why she was preparing for the Civil Services. Not prepared for such a question, she took time to think about it.

"For two reasons."

"As always. Go ahead and state your two-point agenda. I am listening."

"I want to climb the ladder of success in my career without having to wait for years for promotions, the way promotions are usually awarded in the government sector. Secondly, I do not want to get married right away which is what would happen if I gave up."

"Do you prefer transferable jobs?"

"No, in fact that was why I had left my earlier job as I love Delhi too much to leave."

"Do you know that Civil Services carry an all India liability?"

"Yes, I am aware of it, but if one scores low on the merit list, then one can be inducted as a Section Officer and that is a non-transferrable job."

"So, would you leave the Civil Services post if you scored high up on the merit list? Hence, there was always a danger involved. It takes almost two-and-a-half years for the CSE results to be finalized, including police and medical verification. The better idea would be to learn the basics as an assistant. Four years from now, we can appear for the departmental exam for promotion to the same grade of a section officer. There is no danger of getting a transferable job this way."

Shalini thought about it for a while and asked, "What about my second point?"

"Sooner or later, that has to happen. I am sure many of your friends are already married by now. You told me about your friend Raavi. Then why the hitch?"

"I guess because I am scared of marriage. I know people who had to suffer due to dowry problems or domestic violence. I do not wish to get into all that. Then, almost on a daily basis, there are articles in the newspapers about people who had to take loans to get their daughters married off. For them, having a daughter must definitely have been a curse. I would never want to become the reason for my parents' suffering."

She sounded thoughtful.

Kartik pointed out that although that was a good reason to be scared of marriage, still, there was no dearth of good people. Shalini argued that there must definitely be good people around, but judging them in a meeting or two just because they were not asking for a dowry at that point of time, was not possible. Who knows who might burn his newly-wedded wife the very next day!

He reminded her of the Sixth Sense Theory propounded by her which according to him could be of use, if applied at the right time. It may be an hour long meeting or N number of meetings or maybe through verification of antecedents, but a person can certainly be judged.

They discussed the matter at length, but when they realized that they were the only ones talking and everyone else had already gone to sleep, they decided to end the discussion. Before going off to sleep, Shalini requested Kartik that as it was Raavi's wedding the day after, she wanted to make a call the next day.

They could sleep only for four hours before they reached HPF. HPF was around five kilometres from Ooty Railway Station and covered a large area of three hundred acres. The visit to HPF was one of the group's industrial visits, an important component of their study tour. HPF specialized in producing top quality X-ray Films and other such products.

It was situated at such a height that many of them had to take out their warm clothes. They asked the employees of the production unit a lot of questions and the employees were equally cooperative in their quick responses.

They stayed there for three hours after which they were taken to the TTDC Hotel in Ooty. They were told to rest well so that they could go out sightseeing in the evening.

$\mathcal{S}$halini got up at about 5.00 p.m. but was still feeling too lazy to move around. As she was hungry, she managed to go out to the restaurant area to check if someone was around. She could only see Aman. She asked him about the others and was told that Sir had tried, the intercoms of all the rooms, but as everyone was tired, they had been unwilling to go anywhere. He also told her that he and a few others were going out to the local market in an hour.

Shalini requested Aman to give her a call when they were leaving and went back to her room. She called Kartik on his intercom but no one answered. She went out and knocked on his door, but still nobody answered. She could hear that the television was playing loudly and she could hear a few boys laughing. She went back to her room and cried her heart out. She was having mixed emotions: feeling left out, homesick, hungry, tired and last but not the least, sad at not being able to attend Raavi's wedding.

Sometime later, she forced herself out of the bed and washed her hair, then put on a nice t-shirt and capris. On her way to the restaurant, she again knocked on Kartik's door, but to no avail. Unfortunately, dinner was not ready in the hotel's restaurant yet, so she went out of the hotel to have a stroll, but could not find anyone there either. She decided to still go out and enjoy herself on her own for she was a grown woman and could take care of herself. She went back to inform Sir and found Aman and a few others asking for permission to go out.

They decided to walk down to the market area. Just when they were about to leave the hotel gate, Kartik saw Shalini from the window of his room and was perturbed to see that she had gone out with the others. He thought about it for a moment and convinced his friends to walk down to the local market. Though they were unwilling, everyone agreed and went out, albeit unaware that they were actually following the first group.

Once in the local market, Shalini tried to enjoy herself, clicking some photographs, shopping, calling up Raavi to congratulate her, and speaking to her parents and Uday from an STD booth. Yet that feeling of emptiness or of being excluded or missing out on something was not getting out of her system. Whatever it was, it was painful.

She tasted Ooty's street food. She ventured inside a shop of musical instruments with Aman and told him how much she liked listening to the mouth organ. Just when they were about to leave, they heard someone playing a mouth organ. Shalini looked back and saw Kartik playing the instrument, and suddenly she felt a tingling in her stomach.

Shalini went up to Kartik and said sarcastically that she thought that he was inside his room enjoying himself with his friends. He retorted immediately, "Yes I had been enjoying myself in my room, but I decided to go out with my friends and explore the town just as you did."

Shalini did not quite like the comment and left. Soon, she came back to her room and was mostly sleepless throughout the night. She wanted to yell at Kartik, to tell him how restless she was, but was too egoistic to do that. She wanted to cry but controlled her emotions. On the other hand, Kartik was quite upset at Shalini's rude behaviour and the fact that she had gone out with others. He was unable to understand why she was furious with him, while it should have been the other way round.

"Doesn't she know how much I care for her, how much I like her and maybe love her?

Do I love her? Is this what love is all about?"

◆

The next day, the group visited the Tribal Museum of Ooty, where they were told about the tribes, their culture, religion and traditions. They visited a tribe and spoke to its members thereafter.

All throughout the day, neither Shalini nor Kartik spoke to each other. Kartik did not even sit with Shalini in the bus. Shyamal, who could sense a problem, made use of the opportunity and indicated that his warnings about Delhi girls were proving to be true.

"She will call it quits once she is done with you."

"What do you mean by, 'when she is done with you?'" Kartik was furious.

Shyamal explained that she could only be a friend, not a girlfriend; in fact, no Delhi girl was good enough to be a girlfriend. She was using him as she had no company during the tour. He said the problem was that while she saw him only as good company, he was falling for her.

Kartik chose not to react. Shyamal also told him that attitude-wise both of them were poles apart; while he was introvert, she was an extrovert, always looking for and enjoying adventures. She is against non-vegetarian food, which he loved to have. Further, even their castes would not match, so his parents would never agree to such a relation. Once he had finished, Kartik requested him to just let him be.

Shalini, on the other hand, was upset but was also waiting for Kartik so that they could talk it out. She thought that maybe then, she would get rid of those tingling feelings and the stupid pain in her stomach. However, Kartik did not return to his seat and she sat alone the whole way. Although Aman tried to sit next to her, she told him that she wanted to stretch out on the seat.

Later in the evening, the bus took them to Ooty Boat Club, but Kartik and his group stayed behind on the banks of the small lake. Shalini was tired of waiting for Kartik; she strolled alone along the bank for some time, but found she was too weak to control her tears after a while, so she joined those who had got onto a boat. Neither of them knew whether they were trying to avoid each other, or waiting for the other one to make the first move. Once back at the hotel, Shalini went straight to her room. She sat there thinking and sobbing over what was happening to her. She decided that she should just go back as she was probably feeling homesick.

Suddenly, her intercom buzzed. She knew it must be Sir calling her for dinner. She picked up the receiver and heard Kartik's voice instead.

"Hello," said Shalini.

"Shalini what are you up to? Why are you doing this?" Kartik was angry, yet wanted to know what was happening.

"I don't know, I just don't know anything, don't talk to me," she said. Unable to hold herself back any longer, she kept down the receiver. Kartik ran to her room without a second thought. She opened the door. "Why have you come here? Go and enjoy yourself with your friends." She sat down on the bed, wiping her tears.

Kartik sat down near her on the floor. Once she stopped crying, he asked her what the problem was and why she was crying. He was angry, but seeing her cry made confusion take over his anger. In all this, he found her very vulnerable too.

"I never wanted to come for this training. Everyone here has their own set of friends. I am the odd one out. If I had female company, then the case would have been different. You people went out in Rameswaram. Nobody, not even you, asked me if I wanted to come along. Then I told you on the bus that I wanted to wish Raavi on the 12th, but you conveniently forgot all about it. I was hungry too and nothing was available in the restaurant. I came to your room, called you up on the intercom.... but it's okay if no one cares about me. I had gone out with all of them because I did not want to sit alone in the room watching TV..." Shalini had not completed her sentence, when Kartik interrupted her to add, "Or maybe crying."

"No, it's just that I could not take this anymore. It's fine if others are ignoring me or going their own way, but I never expected this from you. I was hurt," she said in a single breath.

Kneeling, Kartik held her hand, but could not utter even a single word. So much was going on inside him that he was not sure what the right course of action was. He simply requested her to freshen up and come for dinner, and went off. He wanted time alone so instead of going to the restaurant, he went to his own room. Shyamal had already left.

Kartik thought if he was interpreting the situation correctly, then maybe, Shalini had already conveyed her feelings although even she was not very clear about her thoughts. She had no expectations from the others, but from him. Why? The answer was clear.

Now it's my turn. Come on! What am I waiting for? I should not have or maybe now I should not be controlling my own emotions. Let people say whatever they want to about Delhi girls; as far as Shalini is concerned, she is not like the others. She is different. I need to give due merit to our relationship now.

He quickly washed his face and went off to the restaurant. Shalini was already there, her eyes searching for Kartik. After the meal, Kartik asked Shalini out for a walk. Before she could say anything, Shyamal said he wanted to come along. They all went together. Shyamal observed that they had patched up. Kartik however, chose to keep mum. He wanted time alone with Shalini, but it was not going to happen that day. He was patient enough to wait for the bus ride the following day.

Later that night, Shalini realized that the little tingling feeling had suddenly disappeared. She was convinced that her discussion with Kartik was the reason for its sudden disappearance. Communication, no doubt, is the best tension reliever.

The next day, they boarded the bus and were informed by Shankar that they were proceeding to their last destination, Chennai. This would be their last and longest bus journey during this trip. They would reach Chennai via Kanchipuram Silk Factory and Mahabalipuram. Soon most of them, including Shalini, were asleep while Kartik was wide awake and eager to give his shoulder to Shalini to sleep on. But Shalini was careful as always. In between, the bus stopped for a quick breakfast break before it sped along on its way to Kanchipuram.

After breakfast, everyone was awake and busy chatting, but Shalini and Kartik were quiet.

After a few rehearsals in his own mind, Kartik said hesitantly, "Shalini, I wanted to say something."

"Go ahead, I am listening."

He looked straight into her eyes, but she looked away immediately. Suddenly she felt the same tingling in her stomach again. She was unable to understand what the reason was, as everything was back as it had been earlier.

Kartik requested her to look at him.

"Why?" she asked while still grappling with the tingling feeling.

"Why not? I am talking to you, and want you to look at me. What's the problem?"

"Because, I can't... you won't understand."

"But I want to understand."

"I don't know why but I have suddenly started getting these tingling feelings in my stomach, when I look at you."

"What is that?"

"Kind of cramps in the stomach, and please don't ask me to elaborate."

"Do you know why you are getting them?"

"No, but I have had such feelings earlier, too..."

Kartik's heart nearly sank on hearing this. He urged her to finish her sentence.

"...Whenever I am about to get an important result for which I have worked really hard, like class X or XII results and the results of our CGL exams, I get such cramps. I wonder what is going to happen now and for how long I will have to suffer like this," she replied quite naively.

"Maybe this time it's the result of the exam called life," he said smilingly, held her hand and continued in a single breath without blinking, saying that may be their togetherness was causing these cramps. Whatever the final result of this exam was to be, the one thing that he was sure of was that he would give it his best shot.

Shalini wondered if her cramps were any indication of her feelings for him. Did that mean she was in love? Still holding her hand, Kartik waited for an answer, but saw that she was lost in her own world. They remained like that till they reached Kanchipuram.

The bus halted for half an hour at a small cotton and silk factory. They visited the production unit where electronic looms were installed, guided the whole way by the owner. Later they were taken to the factory's sales outlet which had a collection of silk saris and cotton shirts.

Shalini bought a silk sari and two shirts with a very slight colour difference between them. Once inside the bus, Kartik asked her the reason for buying two similar shirts. She replied, showing him the shirts that there was a slight colour difference between the two; one was bluish green and the other was greenish blue.

He wanted to know who would like to own such a collection of two shirts that were not exactly the same colour, hoping blissfully that at least one was for him.

"Why are you so eager to know?" she asked with a twinkle in her eyes.

"It's fine if you don't want to tell me," he replied trying to show that he was unaffected. Yet he could not wait any longer and asked her again.

Even she could not resist telling him, and said, "One is for my brother. The other one is meant to be a gesture to wish someone the best. I am going to wait for the final results of the exam called life with that someone. I am with you in this exam."

She handed over the bluish green shirt to him which he immediately put into his rucksack.

"Shalini, why do you get these feelings in your stomach? They are feelings, and feelings are a matter of the heart and not the stomach. So you should logically feel the tingling in your heart."

"Maybe I have swallowed my heart and it's in my stomach too," she said making him laugh loudly.

They reached Chennai at 10.00 p.m. and went to their respective rooms. Although they would miss this bus journey where they had been sitting and holding hands, for Kartik and Shalini the best part of their journey called life had just begun.

They noted that although they had stayed in this hotel earlier, this time it appeared to be more mystical. Out of all the TTDC Hotels in the state of Tamil Nadu, the one in Chennai was the best. Maybe their declaration was making things appear more beautiful to them. After experiencing two sleepless nights, Shalini was finally at ease and slept throughout the night, while on the other hand, Kartik could not sleep. Everything around him had suddenly changed. He had made the biggest and probably the toughest resolution of his life so far. He had moved on from a state of indecisiveness to a state of finality, but he knew he would have to face a lot of opposition and criticism.

Early the next morning, Kartik called up Shalini at 6.00 a.m. and asked her to be ready as they were to leave in an hour. Shalini was already awake. By 7.00 a.m. she was set to move out when she heard a knock on her door. Kartik was standing outside.

"May I come in Ma'am?" he asked jovially.

"Certainly, Sir. In fact I was about to come downstairs," she replied and suddenly noticed the shirt he was wearing.

"Hey, that's the bluish green shirt."

"Yes, and I know that I am looking good."

He took out a rose.

"For you, a very happy morning."

"Will you wake me up like this always?"

"Sure, your wish is my command, Ma'am," he said and bolted the door while saying that.

"Hey, what are you doing?" Shalini asked, becoming defensive.

"Nothing, trust me. I will never do something I should not be doing."

He came near her.

"Shalini, you are looking very beautiful in this blue suit today and I must tell you that this time we are in separate rooms, but I liked this hotel so much that the next time we come here, we will stay in the same room," he said and tried to hug her.

She resisted but gave in hesitantly. However, they soon realized the difference in their heights.

"You are too short," he said and hugged her even more tightly.

"Hmmmm.... So we will make a good pair like Amitabh Bachchan and Jaya Bachchan."

"Oh! Your fixation with Amitabh Bachchan will never go."

Both of them had a good laugh.

An industrial visit to Integral Coach Factory, Chennai was a part of the group's curriculum. They also drove to the Marina Beach. How Kartik and Shalini wished the journey could continue forever!

The study tour ended on the 20th of November, 2002. On their way to Delhi, Shalini and Kartik chose to sit together, prompting a discussion. Despite becoming the centre of attraction, they chose to be themselves and did not try to hide their feelings. Kartik, who used to be a bit cautious, let his guard down. He could not resist being with her, because he knew once this train journey was over, they would be required to answer many questions and face many people.

Shyamal too did not give up on trying to brainwash Kartik whenever he found him alone.

They submitted a report on the study tour and twenty days after that, they had their final exams. After this, everyone reported back to their respective organisations.

On the last day, though, they were let off approximately two hours earlier so Kartik asked Shalini out to Ber Sarai Market for a cup of coffee. They took their cups and sat on a bench.

"Shalini, we are going to report to the office from Monday onwards. I was wondering how we would meet now. Here we were together all the time. There we are posted in different sections and can meet only during lunch. Secondly, I feel people there should not know about us going around because this might create problems for you, since people of all ages and from different backgrounds work there."

"What do you mean Kartik Vats? Are you not sure of our relationship? Do you want to rethink it?" Shalini stood up. Kartik looked around himself to check if anybody was listening, but Shalini was not bothered.

"See, don't flare up at the drop of a hat. I care for you and would not like to hear any indecent remarks about the person with whom I want to spend my life. As far as the surety of our relationship goes, I am very sure about it and I do not, well, cannot rethink it."

Hearing his words, Shalini calmed down.

"First and foremost, I personally feel that only those who are not sure about their relationships try to hide it from society. Additionally, even if we do try to hide it, our batch-mates could spill the beans. Still, if you feel what you think is correct, then I have an idea. During lunch, I will reach Rajpath on my Scooty by 1.15 p.m., which should give you enough time to reach Rajpath too. Then, we can go for a stroll together."

"Tell me Shalini, how many times have you been to Rajpath like this before, because you seem to be having a lot of information about the place?"

"Kartik, you know that I am working in the HR Department. What you might not be aware of is that apart from other qualities, only people with outstanding integrity are chosen for HR, as we have to deal with employees' confidential reports, which often includes our friends' reports too. So, in general, you cannot – and I mean it – doubt my integrity. As far as your question goes, I am a Delhiite, so I have been to Rajpath a number of times with my parents. Anything else that you may like to know, please feel free to ask," she said in a melancholic tone.

"I am sorry Shalini, let's go back..." Kartik realized he was being influenced by Shyamal's ideas about Delhi girls. *I should* trust my girl. Nobody likes to hear comments like these. God! Please help me.

They went back to the ISTM campus to say their final goodbyes to Swamy Sir. Shalini touched his feet and said that it was her dream to be a part of the ISTM as a faculty member some day and that she hoped to become as good a teacher as he was.

He was so touched by her gesture that he said, "Shalini, have I ever told you that you look like my daughter? I bless both of you so you can have a successful career and personal life."

Then he looked at Kartik and told him to always take care of Shalini. Shalini blushed.

Kartik asked hesitantly if he could come to drop Shalini.

"Drop where?"

"Maybe halfway or up to your home?"

"So that you can ensure that I am not going to meet somebody else?" Shalini commented wryly.

"I said sorry, Shalini. I never meant to hurt you."

"Kartik, to me, trust is the most important thing in life. The moment I committed to you, I placed my faith and trust in you. I would never do anything which could create distrust between us and expect the same from you too," she said and left by herself.

Kartik came back to his house and thought about what she had said. He admonished himself for behaving in such an idiotic manner. He could see that whatever she did, she did it whole-heartedly, whether it was a relationship or her career.

It was the 9th of December 2002. All of them joined office and were welcomed by their colleagues. Shalini went to meet Sunaina who looked at her closely.

"How was it Shalini?"

"Oh! Very nice, Ma'am. My exams went well too."

"What about your CSE preparations?"

"Not much progress on that front, I was too busy with the ISTM exams and reports."

"Then why is your skin glowing?" Sunaina teased her.

"Glowing?" Shalini felt awkward.

"Yes, glowing my dear. Is it Dove or love?" she giggled.

"Sunaina ji, please," Shalini pleaded.

"It's okay if you don't want to tell me, but it's written all over your face."

It was lunch time and Shalini's colleagues from her section requested Shalini to have lunch with them. She could not refuse. She observed the camaraderie that eating and sharing lunch brought about between the juniors and seniors.

At around 1.15 p.m., Kartik came in and by mistake dropped a file kept on the corner of a table.

"Shalini, I want to have a word with you."

She finished her food quickly and went to Kartik who was waiting for her patiently after picking up the papers that had scattered when the file had fallen. He, however, noticed that only Shalini's table was neat.

"I have a better idea," he said without waiting for her to speak.

"You wanted to compete for the CSE, so, I will come here at 1.10 sharp. Both of us can study together here. You study for the CSE and as I am really not interested in that; I will either read a newspaper or make test papers for my brother."

She thought about it for a moment. "Did you buy the book on PA only for me?" He hesitated but nodded. "But, later I had decided to appear for the examination."

She smiled, but regained her composure and said that she would discuss this later. "However, I feel that your coming to my section every day would be fodder for the gossipmongers."

"But, we are only studying. Why would people be interested?"

She disagreed.

"If you ask me, I think if we are sure of our relationship and are committed, then we should not be bothered about what others have to say. They might talk about us for a while, but slowly will forget about it if it becomes an everyday routine. As far as the CSE is concerned, I was thinking about what you had told me about the transferable job. Since I have already started the preparations, I do not wish to leave it halfway. So I will give it my best shot for the first and the last time. I request you to do so as well, now that you have already bought the book," she giggled, making him smile too.

"Okay, my dear Shalu," he whispered and chuckled.

"Then let us make a deal: we will study in the afternoons in our respective rooms and will not meet, but I will wait for you near Rail Bhawan at 5.45 p.m. and will come with you to drop you halfway on your Scooty."

"Done. This way people will not see us together."

Both stuck to the study plan for the CSE to be held in May 2003. Kartik would wait for Shalini at Rail Bhawan in the evening and Shalini would arrive on her Scooty. She stayed in a DDA Flat in New Rajendar Nagar, West Delhi. After this, it became a routine for them to drive up to Shankar Road stop or sometimes all the way to Rajendar Nagar.

Kartik would take a bus back to Ber Sarai in South Delhi and in the absence of a single direct bus, had to change buses three or four times. Both of them enjoyed the twenty-minute ride on the Scooty.

Once home, Shalini would change, have her meal and sit down with her books. At first, this was easy, but as the days passed, her concentration began shifting from books to the wonderful Scooty ride. She found it difficult not to think about Kartik. On the other hand, Kartik would reach home by 7.00 p.m. During his bus ride, he too would think of the time spent with her. He realized that Shalini's thoughts were as clean as her table. As soon as Kartik reached home, both the brothers had their meal together and by 7.30 p.m., they'd get down to their respective books. Kartik always had one test paper ready for Dheeraj which he would ask him to work on at 10.00 p.m.

It was the 14th of February 2003. Shalini did not bring her lunch to work on the pretext that there was going to be a promotion party. She called up Kartik on the intercom and informed him that she had a problem to discuss. She asked him out for lunch. He agreed and they met at Mysore Cafe.

Mysore Café was a small restaurant in the South Avenue Market which served South Indian cuisine. It was frequented by government servants who flocked to it during lunch. That day, it was even more crowded because of all the government love birds around.

"Yes, tell me, Shalu, what is it?" Both of them sat on the same seat.

"Tell you what?" she giggled.

"The problem that you wanted to discuss."

"Just wanted to wish you Happy Valentine's Day." She placed a small envelope on the table.

"Come on now, Biharis do not really celebrate this, and ours is not a teenaged love story."

"It's okay if you don't believe in celebrating it, but you cannot say that only teenagers should be the ones celebrating it. Anyone, at any age can enjoy such an occasion."

"Okay. My dear Shalu, tell me what is it?" he said while opening the envelope. Shalini insisted that he open the envelope only after going back.

"But, I haven't got anything for you."

"Your presence in my life is a gift in itself," she replied and started laughing suddenly. "A mushy dialogue, I believe," she explained and continued, "Kartik, why did you buy the PA book for me, as early as in July?"

Kartik was not expecting such a question.

"Actually, hmm…"

He did not know what to say. She watched him carefully; he was blushing and his mind raced to think up a suitable reply.

"To tell you the truth, I admired you from the very beginning. I don't think any of our choices or habits match. Like I have a laid back attitude, while you are such a go-getter; even our eating habits do not match; but the more I know you, the more I fall for you," he revealed while holding her hand and sliding his fingers against hers.

Shalini's heart started thumping so loudly that even he could hear it.

"What happened, Shalu?"

"Oh nothing, nothing at all." She just pulled her hand back and felt the same tingling in her stomach again.

That night she resolved that she would never meet him alone, at least not till they were through with their CSE, as he did something which made her go weak every time. Having said that, she had started liking the little tingling now, although she got nervous at the same time.

Meanwhile, Kartik read her letter as soon as he reached office.

Dear Kartik,

When I see people around falling in love and doing all sorts of stupid things, I feel happy that I am with a sensible and level-headed guy. Hope to be friends first, always.

Yours only,
Shalu.

It was the 20th of March 2003. Kartik had decided to pick up Shalini halfway from the office in the morning. They used to do this when they couldn't finish their discussions during their drive the previous evening. He used to get down approximately one kilometre away from the office building. This time the topic of discussion was vegetarian food versus non-vegetarian food.

"Vegetarian food is healthy food. There are vegetarian substitutes for everything and looking at live fishes swimming is far better for the eyesight," Shalini said.

"How can the food chain be maintained if all the non-vegetarians turn vegetarian?" replied Kartik.

They were engrossed in their discussion on their way to the office when suddenly a VIP car with a red beacon light brushed past their Scooty while speeding away on the wrong side of the road. Kartik lost his balance and Shalini fell down, the Scooty falling on her right foot. Kartik remained unhurt. He helped Shalini and immediately took her to a nearby clinic while cursing the VIPs. Her ankle was bleeding. First aid was administered to her. She insisted on going to office as she had a promotion meeting to coordinate at 10.00 a.m. Kartik insisted that she go home.

"Whose home? I won't go to your home," she giggled.

Kartik patted her back for being cheerful in such a situation. Though he was unwilling, he took her to office.

He parked the Scooty and helped Shalini who was now limping into the building. She reached her room and told the SO what had happened with a small twist in the tale, saying that she was the one driving. Her SO told her to go back home. However, Shalini insisted on being a part of the meeting.

Once the meeting was over, she took a pain killer as the pain had really increased. During the day, she received many calls on the intercom from Kartik who wanted to ensure her well-being. Sunaina heard about the accident and came to meet her friend. She was impressed that in spite of the injury, Shalini had managed to reach office and had successfully arranged the meeting. Shalini felt happy and said that it was always duty first for her.

"But how did you manage to reach office?"

"Ma'am..." And Shalini hesitated.

"Shalini, come on! I want to hear the truth from you."

However, Shalini was not willing to give away her little secret. Sunaina insisted. When Shalini still did not say anything, Sunaina told her that she was from Deoghar and paused for Shalini's reaction.

"So...?" Shalini was clueless about what reaction was expected of her.

"There are a few others who stay there. Find out."

Suddenly, the intercom buzzed again and the SO called Shalini. Shalini almost felt like she had been caught red-handed since she knew that it was Kartik's call.

"Go and ask," Sunaina winked.

"Hello," said Shalini. Kartik asked her for the tenth time how she was doing.

"Fine. Kartik, what is your native place?"

"Deoghar. It's a beautiful place and has one of the jyotirlingas."

"Okay! I will talk to you later."

Shalini was undecided about what she was going to tell Sunaina ji. Looking at her face, Sunaina knew that Shalini had received an answer. Shalini was quiet. "Take your time, Shalini. You can talk to me whenever you feel comfortable."

Shalini was now tense and in pain and she waited anxiously for the day to get over. At 5.30 p.m., Kartik called up again to check if she was comfortable driving to Rail Bhawan.

"No, but, you wait outside the office," Shalini whispered. Although her ankle was swollen, she managed to drive her Scooty till the office gate from where Kartik took over. While driving, Kartik said that half the office had probably seen them together now. Shalini did not reply.

Kartik apologized again for being the reason for her pain. Without understanding what he was saying, Shalini asked Kartik why he had never told her that he was from Deoghar. Kartik stopped the scooter near Rajendar Nagar bus stop.

"You never asked me, and what is the problem? Do you know what a good place it is? Far better than Delhi at least," he said vehemently.

Shalini requested him to drop her near her house. Kartik knew that she was probably in extreme pain, or else she would never have allowed him to come so close to her house. While going back, he was trying to figure out what was going on in her mind.

Once home, Shalini's father immediately took her to the orthopedician. There was a fracture in her ankle and half of Shalini's leg was plastered. This made her immobile. She would not be able to attend office for the next fifteen days. She informed her SO about the problem and took leave.

Late at night, she was unable to sleep because of Sunaina ji's concern. What if Kartik was from Deoghar? Did Sunaina ji know something about him? Something fishy? Shalini knew she would be able to solve the mystery only once she was back at work.

The next morning, Kartik called her up. Fortunately for him, Shalini picked up the phone herself. He greeted her. "Hello Kartik, sorry, I will not be able to come to office today," she said in a formal tone. He asked if her parents were around. When she said yes, he decided to call later.

"Shalu, I do not talk to you much during office. However, just being aware of your absence is making me feel uncomfortable. I am missing you," he whispered from his section later in the day.

"I understand."

"Is there still somebody around you?"

"Uday is sleeping in the other room."

"Tell me, have you studied anything so far? You should make the best use of this time as there are less than two months left for the CSE."

"Yes, I am trying my best."

"Shalu, I am feeling guilty that because of me you'll have to take so many days off."

"Don't worry. It's okay! I think the circumstances are to be blamed for it, not you."

Kartik knew that something was amiss. She was not her usual self.

"No, you are not okay. You are always so happy, so…anyway… I want to meet you. When can I come?"

"It's okay! Please don't come here. What will I tell my parents?" Shalini sounded worried now.

"Why? Haven't your friends ever visited you for group studies?" Kartik tried to reason.

"Yes, they have, but in the presence of my parents and to study. It was different then as I was confident and sure of the reason why the friend was coming home."

"And now you are not sure? Wait, let me guess, about me or about the reason or about yourself. You naughty girl," he chuckled.

"Please try to understand. What will I tell my parents?"

"Don't worry. Just request your mom to come home early tomorrow. By four o'clock."

Oh God! Now what am I supposed to do? What should I tell my mom? That Kartik is coming. Kartik who? My boyfriend? No...I can't do this. Then? Suddenly hundreds of thoughts were flooding her mind.

Why am I so worried? He is going to come here to study. I should not be worried. God, this is even more stressful than a fractured ankle.

In the evening, she requested her mother to come home early the next day.

"Why?" her mother asked, while chopping okra for dinner. Shalini took away the okra and said that till she was at home, she should be given the duty of chopping vegetables. Her mother told Shalini lovingly to concentrate on her exams. Shalini insisted that this would prove to be a good break as she couldn't even move around.

"Okay, but why do you want me to come early tomorrow?"

"One of my colleagues, Kartik, is also preparing for the CSE. He will come home for a study session. At around four," she said in a single breath. Her mother assured her that she would try to do as asked.

The next day, Kartik reached Shalini's home at the right time. Her mother was already there. He came in and touched her mother's feet and said, "Pranam". Her mother blessed him and was rather impressed.

Kartik noted that the DDA flat had small, neatly kept rooms. He was carrying his books and Shalini's mother took him directly to her daughter's room. Shalini was sitting in her pyjamas and a top, her leg in a plaster. Shalini greeted Kartik. He realized that her room had everything in combinations of blue-green; the curtains, the bed sheet, even her study table and walls had cards and bookmarks in the same colour combination.

They started with current affairs directly without further formalities and covered a lot. However, both of them had their hidden agendas ready. Shalini's mother came back with some tea and biscuits. The couple completed quite a bit of work and Kartik left just before her father was to arrive. Before leaving, he told her that he had already taken permission from the office and would come every day.

"What did you tell your SO? That my Shalu is not well?" she chuckled.

"No, I have told him that I can't live without seeing her for even a single day. So they dare not stop me from leaving early," he winked.

Kartik went to see Shalini's mother, and requested her to allow him to come every day at around the same time, so that he and Shalini could revise the entire syllabus. Her mother agreed. When he left, her mother came to Shalini's room and asked her if she was benefitting from the session. Shalini insisted that they had already revised current affairs that day, and would be able to complete the whole of general studies in the next fifteen days.

"Is he not the same guy who was helping you with your luggage in the train?" her mother asked. Shalini nodded.

"But, beta, I may not be able to come home early every day.

"Mamma please, it's only a matter of nine working days. The rest of the days are holidays."

"Okay! I will try."

When Kartik arrived the next day, Shalini's mother was not there. Shalini came limping out and opened the door.

"Hi Shalu, why did you open the door? Is your mother not home?"

"No, she is just about to come back."

"Okay! Then just give me a hug." He hugged her and literally swept her off her feet.

"I missed you, Shalu," Kartik said finally as he took her back to her bed, and sat near her on a chair.

Shalini smiled back. "Let us start with science today." She quickly opened her book and took her eyes off Kartik as the tingling had already begun.

"No, first you tell me, what is it about Deoghar?"

"I think we should not waste our time."

"No, it's important. I insist."

"Kartik, a few people in the office are aware of our relationship now. One of them told me that you are from Deoghar and offered me help as I might need it," she told him earnestly.

Kartik stood up, kissed her on her forehead and said, "Just tell her, whoever she is, that you trust your Kartik and that she should not worry about you."

Shalini felt better and even more confident about their relationship. Both of them sat down and completed their science work that day. Shalini's mother reached an hour later. It soon became a routine. Kartik came on Saturdays and Sundays, too, for even longer time in her father's presence. In fifteen days, they did manage to revise the whole General Studies syllabus.

Shalini re-joined work on the 7th of April, 2003. Although the ankle had healed, there was a little pain and she was still limping. Shalini was overwhelmed by the warm response she received in her office. Kartik came to meet her during lunch. He pretended to have met her after a long time.

"How are your preparations going?" she winked at him.

"Oh! Not much progress and PA is still a problem. Wish I could discuss the main points with somebody," he replied.

Shalini's SO was listening to this conversation. He informed Kartik that even Shalini had taken up PA, so he could join her and they could study together.

"Is it so, Shalini? Then both of us can discuss and study the subject?" He took up the opportunity gladly. Shalini agreed happily. The next day onwards, both of them studied together during lunch. That definitely raised a few eyebrows.

Later that day, Shalini met Sunaina.

"Hello, my dear. It's so good to see you after so many days," said Sunaina.

"Sunaina ji, I wanted to speak to you regarding...." But then Shalini hesitated.

"Don't hesitate Shalini," Sunaina replied as she tried to help her along.

"What help were you talking about? Do you foresee any problems or do you know something about the past?" Shalini enquired.

"Oh! Don't worry. Since both of us are from Deoghar, if you want to get his credentials verified or any other information, then I might be able to dig it up for you. As far as help is concerned, both of you belong to different communities and castes. There, the people are strict about all this, so it might be really difficult for you."

"Thanks for your concern, Ma'am. I will definitely come back to you if and when help is required, but I really wish to know how you came to know about it."

"I am an HR person and these are called tricks of the trade which you will also learn very soon. I wish the best for you, Shalini," added Sunaina and smiled.

During the couple's study session that day, Shalini wrote on a piece of paper, "Kartik, you don't seem to worry about what others will say because your coming here every day is definitely giving rise to speculation."

"Just could not live without seeing you every day. Let people say what they want to... I really do not care," he wrote back.

"Wow...my attitude is rubbing off on you," Shalini wrote in reply.

"Yes indeed... my dear Shalu," Kartik responded in writing.

The chits kept on being passed without Kartik or Shalini changing their expressions. They were definitely not studying. When they were not able to complete their conversations during lunch, they would write letters to each other in a noting format, the official way to communicate, and exchanged these letters during their evening drive.

In one such noting, Kartik wrote,

No: A/LOVE FOREVER @ RAJPATH/2002

1

Refer our conversation dated 15th April 2003.

2. It is clearly evident from the noting under reference that you are very much in love with me and vice versa. However, this is to bring to your kind notice that Rajpath is flanked by the North and South Blocks and we are surrounded by our relatives and friends who might block our way. Nonetheless, the way it finally reaches the gates of Rashtrapati Bhawan, we will also reach our destination of being together some day. After all, as they say, Rajpath is the King's Way, and our love on Rajpath will lead us to togetherness.

3. Submitted for approval please.

Kartik Vats
Assistant

Shalini Pahilajani
Assistant

She wrote back on the same noting:

2

Reference preceding Note.

2. The undersigned agrees with every word of the Note above. Hence, it is,

Approved…As proposed."

It was evident that though they were attempting the CSE 2003, their seriousness towards their relationship outweighed their seriousness towards the exams. This went on till the end of April, when both of them decided that they would go on leave for the exam scheduled for 18th May 2003. However, Shalini was granted leave only for the last five days before the exam. So, despite her efforts to convince him, Kartik refused to go on leave before that. They did try to salvage the sinking ship, although both were sure of their results. They did not even try to study for the mains after the prelims.

A few days later, Shalini got a call from Raavi, who lived in Mumbai. She told Shalini that she was coming to Delhi on the 25th of the month. They decided to meet then.

"I have really missed you, our conversations on trivial topics, our funny gifts..." Shalini was even more excited than Raavi when the latter came to meet her.

"Mohak has gone to Noida to his brother's place for two days so we can enjoy a girls' night out at my mom's.

"I will show you my photographs," Raavi said excitedly.

"Okay let me confirm with Mummy first."

"I'll ask her," Raavi insisted.

Shalini's parents were sitting in the drawing room. Raavi asked them if she could have a stay over with Shalini.

"Raavi, you know that you don't need to ask. You are a part of our family. Tell me, how is your husband?" Shalini's father asked.

"Thanks Uncleji. Mohak is fine."

"Raavi, now that your friend is free after all her exams, just try to convince her to get married. I think you would be the best person to be able to do this." Shalini's father was concerned.

"Sure, Uncleji. I will. Please don't worry."

Raavi was about to leave when Shalini's father asked her if Shalini had somebody in mind.

"Definitely not, Uncleji, or else she would have told me about it," Raavi tried to convince him.

"Yeah, I know that. Okay, go and enjoy yourselves."

Shalini was all ears outside the room. She wanted to inform Raavi of the development in her life but was hesitant. Later that night, when Raavi had already shown Shalini her photographs and was narrating some of her experiences, she suddenly asked Shalini, "So Shalini what's his name?"

"Whose name?"

"Come on, now. Don't act so innocent. You are my childhood friend. I know you better than anyone else. Tell me honestly, quickly."

"Kartik," revealed Shalini.

"Hmmm...I am hearing this name for the first time. Go on and tell me everything from the beginning." Raavi said like an experienced mentor.

Shalini told her everything, from how they had met to their declarations. Once her story was over, she asked Raavi how she had guessed.

"When your best friend is telling you something and you are lost in your own world, then it is quite evident, isn't it?"

As Shalini blushed, Raavi asked, "Shalini, you have not told me when the two of you professed your love for each other. I mean when did you say those three magical words?"

"No, we haven't yet. I feel that it should come from within. Whenever that happens, it will be spontaneous, not planned." Shalini sounded wise.

"When? On your first night together," said Raavi and both of them started laughing.

Later Shalini asked Raavi how she could go about revealing such a big secret to her parents, as that appeared to be a huge task.

"Discuss this with him first, that is, if you people are serious about taking it a step further." Raavi was sceptical.

"What do you mean, Raavi?" Shalini frowned.

Raavi tried to pacify her and said that there had been numerous cases where people were not serious about the relationship.

"Having said this, I am not saying that you will be like them. On the contrary, I am sure of you, but I will be sure of him only once I meet him. So, first and foremost, arrange a meeting. I will come with Mohak but will not tell him anything, so that he can give his independent judgement. You bring Kartik to a place without giving him any prior information."

Shalini nodded and said that they could meet at Mysore Cafe the coming Saturday.

On Friday, Shalini told Kartik that the evening drives were too short and lasted only for twenty minutes. "I wish we could meet tomorrow."

"Our wishes are quite similar, Shalu. Let us meet tomorrow."

They decided to meet at Mysore Cafe just as Shalini and Raavi had planned.

Accordingly, she lied to her parents saying that she was required to go to the office the next day for a few hours. Kartik and Shalini reached the designated place on time. A few minutes later, Raavi and Mohak arrived and pretended to be surprised to see them.

Shalini introduced Kartik as a colleague.

"Hello, I am Shalini's friend, Raavi, and this is my husband Mohak."

Raavi made it easy for Shalini by introducing herself and her husband.

"I have heard a lot about you, Raavi," said Kartik.

They sat in that small shop and ordered coffee and some pakodas. They talked about a lot of things, although nothing specific about the relationship.

Once they had ordered, Raavi said that she wanted to have some more pakodas. Kartik offered to place another order but Raavi insisted that she did not want him to buy more and to just pick up a few from the plate on the counter behind him.

Since it was a small shop, the fried pakodas were immediately placed in a huge plate and brought to the big table kept at the reception for display.

Kartik looked around carefully and when he was sure that nobody was watching him, he picked up a handful from behind him. All of them came out of the restaurant laughing together. Raavi and Mohak left. Kartik and Shalini decided to walk along the Janpath Street Market and have paneer kathi rolls from Depaul's, the famous eating joint in the area.

Later that day, Shalini and Raavi exchanged notes on the phone.

So, what is the verdict, my dear?

My verdict...well it's a long list... a few observations Mohak and I made...

Number one, Mohak guessed that you two were in a relationship as both of you only had eyes for each other.

Number two, I must admit that although we have been childhood friends, I noticed for the first time that you have such beautiful eyes which say so much. Please don't make it so obvious.

Shalini simply could not help but blush hearing this.

Number three, you probably did not notice, but Kartik paid the bill for the stolen pakodas too, although the shopkeeper was unaware of it, indicating Kartik's honesty. So, it's a thumbs up from me and Mohak.

Shalini thanked her but added that she was already confident of the conclusions that they had drawn.

Go ahead and talk to your respective parents, Raavi signed off.

It was August. One Saturday, Kartik and Shalini met at the Mysore Café and Shalini took this opportunity to speak to Kartik about revealing their relationship to his parents.

"Shalini, I wanted to show you something." Kartik took out an inland letter from his pocket, without answering her.

Shalini read it out. It was a handwritten letter from Kartik's father, Shri Vishnudhar Vats, a retired principal of a private school. He was a learned man, and wrote motivational letters to all his students to guide them about worldly matters.

The letter was addressed to Kartik. His father had written that he understood that Kartik had worked hard to get this job. However, he emphasized that to maintain it, even more effort had to be put in.

"You should be in the office five minutes early and should only leave five minutes after office hours. If you wish to sleep peacefully, no work should be left pending. Above all, you should not cheat anybody, and should be honest to yourself. In addition, keep in mind your responsibility towards your younger brother."

Shalini felt that it was indeed a very encouraging letter. Kartik explained that his father wrote whenever he wanted to share his thoughts and that Kartik had a collection of all his letters.

"Can I read all of them?"

"Sure, why not?" He was pleased to see Shalini's interest.

"I have certain queries upon reading this," she replied.

"Hmm... please ask, Ma'am," he answered jokingly.

"What is Dheeraj preparing for?"

"Exams for government jobs."

"What do the rest of your brothers do?"

"My eldest brother is a teacher in Kendriya Vidhyalaya (KV) in Ranchi and the second one is a teacher in the Army. Both of them are married. The third one is an accountant in Bhagalpur in the Bihar Government and he is not married yet. I have an elder sister too, who is also married to a government servant."

"Amazing. So your entire family is into government jobs. But, why do you people lay so much stress on a government job while your father himself has retired from a private school?"

"That's the current trend in Bihar. People get a good match only when the boy has a government job."

"What do you mean by a good match?"

"By good match, I mean good dowry. Fathers want to get their daughters married to a boy who is in a government job, even if he is a Lower Division Clerk (LDC) and the dowry amount rises considerably with the designation. All the boys too want government jobs because they are considered to be stable jobs and...."

"Or may be because it will fetch them a good dowry," Shalini completed his sentence.

"Yes, definitely, that's a big reason as dowry obtained by the son is passed on to the daughter of the house," he replied without a trace of embarrassment or hesitation.

"And, if there are no daughters in the family or they are already happily married, then?"

"Then, that dowry could be used mostly by the newlyweds themselves or if there are any unmarried nieces, cousins, etc., then a chunk would be passed on to them too."

"By that standard, what is that dowry value of an assistant. I mean, what is your value?" she asked directly.

"The day a boy in our state gets a government job, he automatically enters into the marriage market, even if it is without his knowledge. In my case, my elder brother's marriage is still pending, so I think I have not been evaluated so far," Kartik joked.

"Why is your brother not married, considering he already has a government job?"

"His case is strange to my understanding. I do not know what he is looking for in a bride. So far he has already rejected close to six girls. Sometimes it is because of the dowry amount, sometimes the girl's features."

Shalini kept quiet for a moment, as if trying to gauge how to ask her next question, when Kartik said, "I know, what you wish to know. Just like you, I am against dowry and demanding anything is just out of the question. However, after receiving this letter from my father where he has once again reminded me of my responsibility towards Dheeraj, how can I tell him about you? Also, my elder brother is not married yet. So, I will have to wait."

"Yeah, but we can at least inform our parents, otherwise mine may start searching for a match. When I inform my parents, then they will definitely want to meet you and your parents. In that case, you will have to inform your parents too. So, it is better that you inform them in time."

"Don't worry. I will manage everything, just like a true manager. Give me some time. One of my elder brothers, brother number two, Naveen Bhaiya, lives in Shankar Vihar. I will first convince him. Let's see," he said thoughtfully.

While Shalini was wondering if Kartik was really genuine, Kartik on the other hand was scared of making the revelation.

Shalini was tense when she reached home. Suddenly the phone rang. It was her Bua from Agra calling Shalini to Agra for a change. Shalini thought that an escape from the situation for a few days was not that bad an idea. She planned her journey for the 15th August, a Friday, and sought her parents' permission. They agreed readily. Shalini booked her ticket and informed Kartik of the trip on the 14th of August during their evening drive back home.

"What? When are you going?" Kartik stopped the scooter on the side of the road.

"Tomorrow, early morning."

"For how many days?"

"Two days. I will be back on Sunday."

"No, I cannot let you go for two full days. How will we meet on Saturday?"

"Kartik, I am giving you time to speak to your brother, that is, if only you wish to." Shalini pretended to be sarcastic, although she was secretly happy to see that Kartik was feeling desperate.

"Oh! So that was your hidden agenda. But, that's blackmail. Come on, Shalu. I would have informed them even if you weren't going," he said disappointed.

Just then, he seemed so cute and loveable to Shalini that she felt like hugging him and caressing his silky hair.

But they were on the roadside. So, she simply said that once she reached, she would call on the mobile which Kartik had kept with Dheeraj.

The next day, Shalini's father accompanied her to the railway station. This was her maiden journey alone but she did not feel a trace of nervousness. In fact, she now had the time to think about her relationship. She saw people around her – passengers, hawkers, kids going to see the Taj Mahal with their parents – but nothing interested her. She immersed herself in her own world.

She tried to convince herself that though they had only known each other for a year, she trusted him to the core. "Or else why would I have allowed him to touch me? I just need to be patient. I know nothing will go wrong."

Kartik, on the other hand, was trying to think of a way to tell his brother his love story. He first spoke to Dheeraj about it. Dheeraj, who had completed his education in the village, had a rigid attitude.

He said, "Bhaiya, I don't know what to say. I am sure Bade Bhaiya will never agree. The girl might be very nice but our traditions and customs do not allow this."

Kartik was annoyed as he had not been prepared for this. "What rubbish, Dheeraj? What do you mean by such a thing? I love her and want to marry her. Our elders might have this attitude, but I never expected such a reaction from you."

"Bhaiya, please calm down. These are not my views. I am only echoing the views of our elders. You will have to be prepared for opposition, as yours is the first such case. I will obviously stand by you, but how will you convince the others?" Dheeraj replied as he explained his stand.

Kartik's tone mellowed as he apologized for his behaviour. He had not been prepared for any kind of opposition and felt that he should start getting ready for it. In the afternoon, he waited for Shalini to call, but she did not. He guessed that she was probably stuck with her relatives. He was not at peace and his restlessness was growing. He decided to go and meet Naveen Bhaiya in Shankar Vihar and took Dheeraj's mobile with him.

Once there, he went straight to his Bhabhi and took her to another room.

"Bhabhi, I want to speak to you; it's urgent."

His Bhabhi was a jovial person. She was thrilled to hear that her young brother-in-law was in love with somebody. Kartik was relieved to see his Bhabhi's excitement. "How should I reveal it to Bhaiya?"

"Oh, you don't worry. I will inform him." And without waiting another moment, she just barged out of the room. Kartik did not dare to go out and waited till he heard his brother calling him.

"What is your Bhabhi telling me? Is it true that you are seeing somebody? Don't you know that Bade Bhaiya will never agree to it and that there have been no love marriages in the family," he said in a stern voice. Kartik kept mum.

Before Bhaiya could say anything else, Bhabhi asked him to show her a picture of Shalini. Kartik immediately took this opportunity, sat beside them on the floor saying that he didn't have one, but could bring her in person if they allowed him to. Before Bhaiya could say anything, his Bhabhi immediately nodded.

Bhaiya asked him what caste she belonged to.

"She is a Sindhi Brahmin, Bhaiya," said Kartik without blinking.

"Who is a Sindhi?" he asked.

"The word 'Sindhi' originated from the word 'Sindhu,' as the community used to live near the river Sindhu. During the Partition, many of them shifted to India," Kartik replied as he passed on the information that he had mugged, and requested him to meet her first.

Bhaiya agreed as he was under pressure from his wife. Kartik was relieved and wanted to share the news with Shalini. It was already 7.00 p.m. He was worried why Shalini had not called him yet. His desperation grew so much that he called up her Delhi residence. Her father picked up the phone.

"Hello Uncle." Kartik was dead nervous, but wanted to share his news with Shalu so desperately that he mustered up all his courage.

"Uncleji, I wanted to speak to Shalini."

"She is not at home, beta. May I know who is calling?"

"I am Kartik, and just wanted to inform her that she has to come to office on Sunday at around eleven. I know that she has gone to Agra. Has she reached?"

"Yes, she has reached. Why are you asking this? Is it something important? Tell me, I will inform her," responded her father.

"No...huh...yes...yes, Uncle, it was important. But it's okay," Kartik said hesitantly.

Shalini, on the other hand, was thrilled to meet her Bua. She was in good and happy company, but secretly wanted to reach out to Kartik. She did not wish to disclose her secret to anyone, so she did not make any calls from her Bua's house. She was trying to devise a plan to call Kartik. Suddenly she saw her Bua's daughter Kirti coming towards her on her cycle. An avid cyclist herself, Shalini asked Kirti if she would like to have a cycle race. Kirti was a young student in class six. She readily agreed. While passing through the market, Shalini spotted an STD booth.

Kirti took her chance first while Shalini noted the time she took. Then Shalini took to the cycle and drove really fast, straight to the market. She thanked God when she saw that there was no queue at the booth. She immediately dialled Kartik's number and realized how happy she was to hear his voice.

"Hello Kartik, Shalini," she said excitedly.

"No, you are not Shalini; you are my Shalu."

Shalini went red and could not say anything because the tingling feeling had started all over again. Both of them exchanged quick notes. While Shalini informed Kartik that she was calling from a local STD booth, Kartik told her about how his elder Bhaiya and Bhabhi had agreed to meet her. He also informed her about his call to her father so that she would be cautious.

"Okay, take care and good night," Shalini said.

"My days and nights are not good without you now. I want you with me, especially now that I have got a positive response from one of my brothers."

"God! Even I miss you. But bye for now or else they might send a search party for me. Bye."

She became aware of her surroundings when she saw the time and cycled faster than ever. Kirti was waiting for her eagerly and announced happily that she had won the race as her didi had taken longer than her.

"Good Kirti, I am so proud of you. And yes, tomorrow we will race again and then I will win for sure," said Shalini, realising how happy she was even when she had lost.

Shalini enjoyed her stay in Agra. The next day she did not get a chance to use the same trick because despite her resistance, her Bua took her out shopping. She looked at all the STD booths longingly. All her hopes were dashed when the shopping and sight-seeing, including a visit to the Taj Mahal was over and they returned home.

She had always wanted to see the Taj Mahal, but that day, she was saddened after seeing that.

"How Shahjahan must have missed his beloved that he had a makbara made for her? Even I am missing Kartik very much." Her longing only grew upon visiting the Taj Mahal. She enjoyed herself more at the other tombs where she and Kirti fed a lot of monkeys and langoors.

She wished she could just meet Kartik that very Sunday. She was lost in her own world when her Bua came into the room and asked her if she was asleep. Shalini sat up.

"Shalini, what are your chances of getting through the CSE?" her Bua asked.

"Very bleak," replied Shalini honestly.

"Then, what next? Do you plan another attempt?" her Bua probed further.

"Not yet decided, Bua, but I just wanted to take a break from the routine," answered Shalini cautiously, because she knew that if she said no, then Bua would ask her to get married.

"Even I wanted you to take a break; that is why I called you here. You have been studying continuously for years now. It is a small but a well-deserved break for you. Take this break as an opportunity to decide on your future course of action. I will not tell you to get married right away. But Shalini, you know, you have reached that age and that juncture of life where, after a while, you will look around yourself and find that all your friends have got married. And none of them will have much quality time for you. Then you will feel lonely. So, take some time and decide. Nobody is going to force you to do anything. I will suggest that you start helping your mom in the kitchen. I must tell you, even preparing chapatis and a good Sindhi kadi is like solving a difficult maths problem," Bua explained and Shalini nodded in agreement.

Shalini returned home at around twelve. Her father told her about the call from Kartik and that she was called to the office by eleven in the morning. Before she could say anything, Uday (who was home), offered to drop her to the office. At any other moment, she would have felt happy at being offered a lift, but not in the current situation. She simply refused to go to the office saying she was way too tired and would rather spend the time with her family. She, however, let Kartik know.

The next morning, Shalini woke up to the alarm she had set at five in the morning, freshened up and went to the kitchen to find her mom already making tea.

Her mother was pleasantly surprised to see her. Shalini said that she had decided that from now on, she would get up early every day. She went for a walk with her parents and by 6.00 a.m. was with her mother in the kitchen.

"Now, you tell me what to make and how much to make," said Shalini confidently as she led her mother to a chair she had brought.

"Let me help you, you will not be able to make everything on your own." Her mother stood up.

"Let me try, Mamma, and I won't let you stand at all." Shalini was adamant.

It took her two hours to finish everything. After that she went to her room and lay down on her bed. Her mother came in, only to find Shalini sleeping. She called Shalini's father who looked at their daughter lovingly as she had volunteered to prepare breakfast and lunch on her own for the first time. Her mother then woke her up at around 8.45 a.m.

"Mamma, I am too tired and don't want to go to office today."

"Shalini, you were called on Sunday too but you did not go. Now, you don't want to go on Monday also. This is not done. Do not waste the day. Just be a good girl and get ready".

As her mother turned to leave the room, Shalini immediately got up and hugged her and asked her as to how she managed to do so many things at the same – time and never feel tired.

"Women are good at multi-tasking. I used to concentrate on many things at the same time – like making food in the kitchen, washing clothes in the washing machine and simultaneously keeping an eye on my kids."

"I love you, Mom, and hope to be as good as you at managing my home," Shalini said and hugged her.

Her mother immediately looked straight into her eyes and asked warmly, "Shalini, who is he?"

"Who he?" Shalini was embarrassed.

Her mother sat down and caressed her hair. She asked her gently, "I love you Shalini and have always trusted your judgment. Please answer a simple question, very honestly. Will you?"

Shalini nodded. Her mother was as nervous as her daughter then.

"Do you like Kartik?"

Shalini did not know what to say. She was so shocked at this sudden development that she went numb. She put her head on her mother's lap and could not say much, "Mamma…"

"It's ok, beta. He is a nice guy. Don't feel embarrassed. You are a big girl," her mother tried to comfort her.

"But how did you come to know?"

"Hmmm…that's not important. What is important is, are you sure of your decision?"

"Mummy, you know me very well. I take time to reach a decision, but once I decide, I am quite sure of it."

"So, should I speak to your father?"

"No, no Mummy, please do not jump to the next level. First you tell me, how did you come to know?"

"You never wanted to get married Shalini and suddenly you are hoping to be as good as your mother in 'managing your home'. If that is not quite a signal for your mother then what else could it be, 'my dear Shalu?'" Her mother hugged her.

"Oh Mummy, if you had already heard him call me by this name, then why did you wait for a signal? You could have asked me earlier too." Shalini was still embarrassed.

"I heard him calling you Shalu when he came here to study. You have had friends coming to our place earlier too, but I could see a different expression in your eyes whenever he was around. So I was sure, but was waiting for you to tell me on your own. When you offered to help me in the kitchen, I knew that my daughter was all set to embark on a new journey and fortunately, you gave me a chance to talk to you about this yourself," explained her mother.

"Mamma, please don't tell anybody right now. I will tell you when it's the right time," said Shalini. Suddenly she looked at the clock and rushed out of her room for office.

That day her heart was not in her work. She was itching to meet Kartik to let him know of the development. However, throughout the day, she had her hands full with receipts for which she was required to draft replies urgently.

In the evening, when they could both meet, they were super excited, as both of them had a lot to tell each other.

When she reached Rail Bhawan and saw Kartik standing there, it felt as if it had been a long time since they had met each other. That day, she wanted to hold Kartik tight, but could not muster up the courage to do so.

She, however, held onto his shoulders for the first time while riding pillion. Kartik requested her to come closer. Shalini could not hear. He shouted from inside the helmet that he wanted to tell her something. She tried going closer, but still could not hear much. Kartik stopped the Scooty and told her to sit with one leg on each side of the Scooty like men do so that she could hear what he wanted to say. She obeyed. Once they started their journey again, he pulled her hand against his waist, making her lean on him. Suddenly, she could feel the tingling feeling again.

Gosh! I have forgotten everything I wanted to share with him. He always takes me by surprise.

She tried to pull her hand back, but he refused to let go.

"Look, we have already had one accident, why do you want me to make another mistake? Let me concentrate and be where you are," he said lovingly and authoritatively at the same time.

She requested him to place his hand back on the Scooty's handle as she did not want to stay at home for another fifteen days.

"That's better," Kartik laughed. Shalini asked him what he wanted to say.

"I can't."

"Why?"

"Because the moment you leaned on me and I felt the soft touch of your body, I forgot everything."

He stopped the Scooty at a place different from their usual Rajender Nagar bus stop. Shalini asked him where they had reached and looked around. She realized that they were in Pusa.

"That means you too were engrossed by the touch and fragrance of my body as much as I was by yours. Or maybe even more because I still managed to drive you to the place I wanted, but you did not notice that."

"No, it's not like that. I had closed my eyes so that..." But before she could complete her sentence, Kartik said, "So that nobody can see you... just like a cat."

She turned her back on Kartik, trying to stop herself from blushing and told Kartik to come straight to the point.

"Come on now, Shalu, don't pretend. I was so excited to tell you that I have managed to convince my brother to meet you. We will go there to meet him this Saturday. Tell me, isn't this great news worth a hug? Since we meet only on the road, that was not possible, so I thought this Scooty ride would be a great way to get my priceless hug from you," he said while they walked down the lanes of Pusa, a lustrous green belt in the thick of Delhi.

Shalini informed him that even she had similar news to share.

"Tell me, my dear Shalu."

"My mom knows everything."

"*What?*" he expressed his shock. "*How? When? Why?*"

His expression made her laugh.

"I felt happy that your brother knows and wants to meet me and just look at you and your sad and shocked expression," Shalini answered, pretending to be angry.

"No, I am happy. I just got a little scared. Tell me, when am I supposed to meet her?"

"It's okay, Kartik. Don't worry. Let us go step by step and meet your brother first this Saturday."

It was the 23rd of August, a Saturday. Shalini informed her mother that she was supposed to go to meet Kartik's elder brother. Her mother became tense and said that she could not allow Shalini to go.

"Please Mummy, just this time. After this, I will call him home to meet you. You speak to him and only once you are satisfied we will inform Papa," urged Shalini.

Her mother was reluctant; still she gave in to the request. Shalini wore a light pink suit that day. She was about to put on lipstick, when she remembered how Kartik had told her once, "You are so natural, unlike the other girls who wear all sorts of weird make-up, yet cannot conceal their features. I like you the way you are. Please never wear any make-up."

So she kept her make-up kit down, took her Scooty and zoomed off. They had decided to meet at the office first. As they rode to his elder brother's house, Shalini requested Kartik to stop near a temple.

"Come on, Shalini! Where will I find a temple now? I don't have time for all this," he almost shouted.

"Please stop the Scooty," she said.

"Now what?" He seemed angry, but stopped the Scooty nonetheless.

She asked, "Is there a problem Kartik? Are you nervous? Am I not dressed correctly?"

"There is no problem Shalu, but..."

"But what? I am sure you are nervous. Don't be when I am with you," she laughed.

"I am nervous as hell and you are laughing. That's not done."

"Kartik, just take a deep breath."

This time, she just could not resist and pinched both his cheeks because he looked very adorable. He was surprised at her initiative but it changed his mood completely.

Shalini continued that she wished to bribe the Almighty so that the result of that day's project was positive.

"Oh! So that's the point. Got it, Ma'am. Let's deal with Project Bhaiya via a temple then."

They went to a small temple at the Sarojini Nagar bus stop. A devotee of Lord Shiva, Shalini prayed that their courtship be transformed into a lifelong relationship. While they proceeded on their journey, Kartik went on giving her tips about how to deal with his Bhaiya and Bhabhi. Shalini was scared but dared not show her nervousness to Kartik.

Kartik got a call on his mobile as they were proceeding. He requested Shalini to take the call. It was his brother, Naveen, on the other end. Shalini requested Kartik to stop the Scooty, but Naveen insisted that he wanted to speak to her only. She said, "Namaste Bhaiya," and got down from the Scooty.

"Shalini, I wanted to know your caste," asked Naveen.

"I am Sindhi."

"Sindhi is your language. I want to know your caste," he clarified.

She apologized for having such little or perhaps no knowledge on the subject. Naveen said it was okay, but at the same time, told her not to come to their house as he was not the decision maker in their family.

"A yes from me does not carry any weight as my eldest brother is the decision maker and he will never agree to such a relationship. Since ours is a conservative family, a lot of importance is attached to caste. Obviously, you don't seem to be aware of all these things," Naveen said and disconnected the call. Tears rolled down from Shalini's eyes. She gave the mobile back to Kartik. He could guess what must have transpired from her expression. Shalini narrated the conversation.

Kartik told her as Bhaiya had told her himself that he was not the decision maker, it was useless going to him in any case. Kartik told Shalini to just chill.

He took her to a coffee shop in Sarojini Nagar market. He was very disturbed himself, but he did not let it show. He was feeling suffocated but cheered her up by asking her when he could come for a cup of tea with her mother.

"Thanks," Shalini smiled. He pinched both her cheeks softly.

"Hmmm... what was this for? Am I your baby?" she teased.

"No, you are not my baby, but I want you to become the mother of many, many of my babies," he teased back, making her blush.

"Excuse me, let's go, Kartik. My mom will be waiting for me."

She told him that an interview with her mother would not be much of a worry as she would only ask questions about any bad habits and other general questions. Shalini changed the topic again and explained everything during the drive back.

When she reached home, she told her mother that not much had been asked.

The next week, Shalini got a note from the Estate Office, the office responsible for allotment of government flats to government servants. She was thrilled to go through the contents. She called up Kartik and they decided to meet at Mysore Café during lunch.

He asked her what the matter was. She was happy to share that she had been allotted government quarter in Sarojini Nagar under the single ladies' pool. He read the letter and asked when she had applied for it.

"Before going to ISTM and that too on the suggestion of my grandfather, my Nanu."

"And what are you going to do with it?" Kartik was not excited about it at all.

"Look Kartik, my Nanu had guided me to apply for government accommodation. He knew that it is easier to get a government quarter when a lady is single under the single ladies' pool, but impossible to get it when one gets married. See how correct his speculation was. You live in a rented accommodation. A bachelor's accommodation is obviously different from a family accommodation. Tell me after we get married, can we live in your rented accommodation?"

"Obviously not."

"So we will need a place to live. With our meagre salaries of ten thousand rupees each, we cannot even imagine of buying a place immediately. So, till we are able to buy our own house, a government accommodation and that too, a centrally located one, is better than a rented accommodation any day. What do you say?" she concluded.

"Yeah, that's a very practical thing to do. But, you will lose out on your house rent allowance, a major component of a government servant's salary. Until you get married, even the house remains vacant. Additionally, after marriage, both of us will be losing out on our respective HRAs as per the rules, which would come out to a total of six thousand rupees," Kartik explained.

"That's a small price for a good centrally located house in Delhi," Shalini responded.

"So, that's done then." Kartik paid the bill and they went out. He then took her to meet someone on the Scooty.

"Where are we going?"

"To meet Dheeraj. I want him to support my case when I take it up with my parents."

Shalini met Dheeraj and saw the small one-room rented accommodation where they lived in Ber Sarai. Contrary to her expectations, the house was very neat. Shalini told Dheeraj that in case he had any problems with English, he could call her at any time.

"What should I call you?" Dheeraj asked jovially.

"You decide."

"If it's my call, then I will call you Bhabhi, as I am sure you will definitely become that one day."

Shalini thanked him and the couple left for office.

"Shalini, my eldest brother is very conservative and the rest of my brothers are scared of him. However, even he cannot go against my father's orders. In general, after retirement my father had passed on the reins of decision making to my eldest brother and only in very rare cases he takes a decision himself. If we can influence my father, our union is possible, because I know Bade Bhaiya will not budge," he said while on the way back. Shalini listened carefully.

"Don't worry Kartik, everything will fall into place automatically," she said, though even she was not sure after the Project Bhaiya fiasco.

It took her almost two weeks to complete the formalities for taking possession of the government accommodation. Her father quizzed her about it and while her mother knew the answer, she chose to remain silent on the issue. Shalini, however, replied that it was very difficult to get government quarters, but once it was allotted, one had to accept it although it could be surrendered after proper acceptance. "Nanu had told me to apply for it," Shalini added. She thought that she would at least get some time before she revealed everything to her father.

During their evening drive the next day, Shalini suggested that Kartik shift to the government accommodation allotted to her.

"As per the conduct rules, which all government servants are bound by, I cannot do so unless we declare in the office that I am your legally wedded husband," he laughed.

"Hmmm...then we will have to wait. But now the house is ready to welcome its would-be occupants. So, please tell your brother number three to get married fast."

"Why are you in a hurry to get married?" he teased.

"No, don't be too happy. I am a Sindhi and Sindhis never like to face losses."

"Oh, come on now. I know everything, my dear Sindhi."

Shalini reached home and was told that her father was supposed to go out of station for a few days for some official work on Sunday morning so Shalini's mother told her to call Kartik home on Sunday afternoon.

The next day, after office hours they decided to go to Depaul's, one of their favourite joints. They parked their Scooty in Parliament Street and walked down Janpath holding hands. Shalini told Kartik that her mother had called him for a meeting on Sunday, when suddenly their path was blocked by a young guy of approximately the same age.

"May I know what you are doing here?" the young guy said as he looked at Shalini.

She immediately let go of Kartik's hand on seeing the guy and said that Kartik had wanted to buy a gift for his sister's birthday; he had requested Shalini to help choose a suitable gift. She knew that more questions would follow.

"God please make me evaporate into thin air. I really wish to vanish," she prayed.

"And is that the reason why you were holding hands?" he asked, apparently furious.

"No, actually he suddenly sprained his ankle, so I had to hold his hand, or else he would have fallen."

"Which ankle?" asked Tarun, the young guy. Shalini and Kartik both spoke at the same time, Shalini said 'left' while Kartik said 'right'.

When Tarun looked at her quizzically, Shalini quickly corrected herself and said, "Yeah, it's the right ankle, I was mistaken."

"Then, let me help him...what did you tell me, his name was, Di?"

"Oh, I forgot to introduce the two of you. This is Kartik, we work in the same office; and this is Tarun, Uday's best friend and my rakhi brother." At the same time Shalini was wondering how she could tell him to leave.

"Hello Kartik ji." Tarun helped him while holding him by the shoulder. Kartik acted as he if he was in pain and also limped a bit. Shalini and Tarun made Kartik buy a kurti from Janpath for his 'sister'.

"Di, how is this black one?" Tarun asked.

"No, I think, this pink one would look good on her." Shalini giggled on seeing Kartik's face.

"Kartik ji, what size kurti do you want?"

"The same size would fit her as your di, so we can pick one that suits her." Kartik winked at Shalini.

They bought a pink coloured kurti for her and Kartik did not forget to continue limping till they reached his bike. Tarun offered to drop Kartik. However, Kartik said that he would get a bus from that very bus stop.

Once Tarun had left, Kartik and Shalini went to the same shop again and tried to return the kurti. The shopkeeper refused. Kartik told Shalini that as she had chosen and bought it, so she should keep it. She did and wore it to office the very next day.

However, as fate would have it, Tarun came to meet his dear friend Uday in the evening and saw Shalini in the same kurti. His doubts were confirmed. Before Shalini could do any damage control, the damage was already done. That night, when Tarun left, Uday asked her who that chap had been. She confirmed his doubts and told him everything about Kartik. Uday was also informed by the mother-daughter duo of the upcoming meeting with Kartik.

It is very difficult for a brother to understand and accept that his sister is having a love affair. Uday was clearly annoyed, but bowed down to his mother's orders about the meeting.

Although he was nervous, Kartik reached on time. Shalini opened the door. She looked beautiful in a long skirt and short top.

"Hmmm... not bad, you have never looked so beautiful before," he whispered. Shalini welcomed him. Uday also greeted him and recognized him instantly as the boy who had helped load her luggage on the train during the ISTM trip.

Uday called Shalini inside for a moment and asked her since when had she been going around with the Bihari chap.

"Bhai, please try to understand, what is important is not whether he is a Sindhi or Bihari, but whether your sister will be happy with him or not," Shalini tried to make Uday understand.

"And who will ensure that?" he asked.

"Only the two of us can ensure this with the emotional support and blessings of our respective families."

"Suppose after marriage he shows his true Bihari colours?"

"And what are true Bihari colours?"

"If he beats you up, does not bother about you, might seek a lot of dowry or if his family does not accept you, then..." Shalini interrupted him.

"Tell me, how many Bihari men do you know who have done this to their wives, and I will tell you about Sindhis who do not treat their spouses the way they deserve to be treated. There is

135

no end to ifs and buts. At best I can ensure that if he or any of his family members seek dowry, then I will not marry him. As a matter of fact, I will not marry at all in that case." And with that, she stood up and left.

Uday knew it was impossible to win an argument with Shalini. So he thought of devising other ways to discourage her. In any case, he went to the drawing room to meet the man his sister had chosen. Kartik, on the other hand, was answering Shalini's mother's queries about his bad habits. She was already impressed with him.

Uday asked him, "Kartik ji, what is your zodiac sign?"

"I don't know," replied Kartik.

"Di, he does not even know what his zodiac sign is while you are such a firm believer," Uday said rather sarcastically.

"He is not aware of his birth date, so how will he know his zodiac sign. And it's not important. Please forget about it," Shalini replied angrily.

"Not aware of his birth date? Which era does he belong to? Mummy, how will we get the horoscopes matched if he does not know his birth date? I don't think there is any point in taking this any further." Uday stood up to leave. Kartik requested him to wait and Uday took his seat again.

"I come from the interiors of Bihar. My parents initially used to live in a small village in Deoghar. There was no electricity or even the basic facilities there. We are a big family of six children. Remembering the birth dates of all the children was considered inconsequential. My date of birth as entered in the school and office records is the one decided by my village school principal, that is, 1st March. In fact, as far as I remember, the date of birth of all my siblings is the same, obviously with different years, and has been kept by the school principal only. If I am recollecting correctly, the date of birth of all the kids in my class was 1st March, it being the Budget month," Kartik tried to explain.

"I agree, but we cannot go ahead without tallying the *janampatris,* for which we definitely need the date and time of birth," Uday insisted.

Shalini explained that even Ritu's horoscope had been matched before marriage. "She and her husband were not only perfect zodiac partners but numerologically they were supposed to be the best possible pair ever. Everyone knows what has happened in her case. So what is the sanctity of these things?" asked Shalini.

"Although I agree with Shalu, if Uday still insists on knowing my birth date, I will try to find out, because my mother knows it as per the Hindi calendar *tithis.* However, I would like you to know that two of my brothers and one sister have been married for many years now. None of them know their birth dates, yet all are happy and enjoying their marital lives," stated Kartik.

Shalini went to see him off and apologized for Uday's behaviour. He said that he knew that Uday was just being a concerned brother. He assured her that he would go to his hometown and gather information.

Later Shalini had a terrible fight with Uday. Her mother intervened and told Uday that Shalini's arguments were correct. However, if Kartik could still try to get his correct date of birth, there would be nothing like that.

Uday too tried to pacify Shalini. "Di, if the horoscopes match, then I promise I will be the one convincing others, although I would have been happier if he had been a Sindhi."

Shalini replied that if Uday was genuinely apologetic he could help her buy two mobile phones. Uday was excited to hear that she wanted to gift him a mobile.

"Sorry, but it is not for you; it will be one each for me and Kartik," she clarified.

"Although I don't approve of this, I will still come with you on the promise that if the horoscopes do not match, you will forget him," Uday said. Shalini agreed. Both of them went to the market.

They bought two Reliance phones with interconnectivity for an extra payment of only fifty rupees. Shalini and Kartik could now talk to each other for as much time as they wanted. While Uday was starting his bike, Shalini went back to the shop pretending that she had forgotten her purse there and bought one more mobile for Uday.

Shalini was happy with the purchase, while Uday was hoping that the horoscopes did not match. Once home, she gave the surprise gift to Uday so he would go back to being his normal self.

The next day when they left the office, Shalini requested Kartik they go for a drive to Pusa. Once they reached there, she asked him, "You did not even hesitate once before calling me Shalu in front of my brother and mother?"

"Love has made me strong," Kartik replied.

"How will you get the horoscope made?" Shalini asked.

"I am going there during Durga Puja, I will try to find out from the old records that we have in the house and will ask my mother too," he replied.

"It's okay Kartik. I will give you an easy idea. Just take my date and time of birth, find out from any pandit a matching date and time for yourself," she suggested while strolling around in Pusa.

He stopped immediately and said, "Love has made you blind, Shalu. If I cheat you now, I will cheat you all our lives. Will you ever be able to trust me then?"

"Good, I appreciate your gesture. So, you are entitled to a gift from me." She handed the phone to him. Kartik opened the packet and was surprised.

"It's wonderful, but how much did you spend on this?" he asked.

"It's a gift from me for you and myself too."

She showed him her mobile phone and told him about the special inter-connectivity feature and the unlimited talk time. She also informed him how Reliance was playing the cupid with the fifty-rupees scheme.

"Good, now we can keep in touch. It's the most apt gift in the current situation."

"But Kartik, I don't want you to leave. I will miss you"

"I will miss you too, but it's important so we can be together all our lives."

Kartik reached his village, Deoghar. Although he remained busy, he did not forget to call Shalini at least once a day.

Shalini would miss him most during her drive back home. The feeling, that he was not around made her indifferent to the things around her.

One day, she messaged Kartik,

I do not love you.
But the fact that I am in love is far more lovable.
It makes everything around me just so beautiful.

Kartik read the first line and tears fell from his eyes. He was immediately reminded of what Shyamal used to tell him about how untrustworthy Delhi girls were.

"Is she telling me that she is ditching me? But why? What wrong have I done?" He just could not scroll down and by now had started sobbing hard.

Still after some time he managed to scroll down and read the next few lines. He was still crying, but it was now out of happiness and love for his girl. He called her immediately, still sobbing. "Shalu, did you just say that you love me?"

"No dear, if any such thing has made you cry, then I will never ever say such a thing. Please tell me what has happened?

Did your elder brother disapprove completely? Please tell me or my heart will just jump out of my mouth. Or I will have a severe stomach upset," she said without pausing even once.

"I miss you Shalini. Had it been possible, I would have flown over there."

"You didn't tell me what happened," she insisted.

"Just an overflow of love for you has made me cry. Please kiss yourself from me, I think that is the only remedy," he said lovingly.

"That's your job, Mr Vats. One should not transfer one's job to others. I will keep it pending for you so you can do it on your own."

"Ok then, I will consider it as your permission, so that you can't back out."

They spoke to each other for a few more minutes where he revealed that he was almost on the verge of finding out his date of birth and that everyone knew about Shalini's presence in his life. He told her how much his eldest brother had scolded him and had commanded him to refrain from ever meeting her, but that had made his decision even stronger.

He came back in mid-October and requested Shalini to take a day off and come to her government quarter. She reached there only to see him already waiting for her with a broom and a mop.

"What is all this?" she asked.

"I wanted to clean our house," Kartik told her.

"Our house...hmmm..." she teased.

"Yes, our house, our future house, our future drawing room, our kitchen, our bedroom, our lobby."

"This is such a beautiful feeling. Have you got some positive news from your home? You seem to be excited."

"Yeah, I am excited. But I will tell you the details only once we finish the cleaning," he said enthusiastically.

The two of them took almost two hours to clean all the rooms. They were tired and hungry at the end of it. Kartik went to Sarojini Nagar market and got them something to eat. Once they had had their lunch, Kartik told her that he had so many things to share but most importantly, he told her that he now finally knew his date of birth.

"What is it? Let me guess, you seem to be so level-headed that I feel that you could be a Libran, so is it between 20th September and 20th October?" she guessed.

"Yes, absolutely correct. I am actually surprised to see your knowledge on the subject. No wonder you and your family are so much into these things. My birthday is today, the 16th of October," he told her excitedly.

"My goodness and you are telling me this now. I mean, we have been together for the past three hours and you hid such a big thing from me?" Shalini was even more excited than Kartik.

"My gift please," he asked jovially. She put her arms around his shoulders, and asked, "Tell me, what do you want?"

"You." He pulled her towards himself.

"I am already yours," she responded lovingly.

"What about my pending kiss?"

"If you keep on asking me for it, it may never happen."

"Good to hear that." Then they shared their first passionate kiss.

"Kartik can I see you without your moustache?" she asked mischievously after the kiss.

"No, I can never compromise on my moustache. I love it too much to shave it off," he replied.

"That is your *ghar ki kheti*. You can always regrow it if you don't like your look, but please give it a try at least once."

"Maybe my moustache hurt you, that is why you are insisting," he laughed, embarrassing her.

"It's okay, but I would still like to see you clean shaven someday."

Then, they looked at the house fondly and left for Sarojini Nagar market. On their way to the market, he told her that his parents would be coming to Delhi soon to meet them. They would initially stay with his second Bhaiya and later for a few days with him. He felt, it would be the most opportune time. He told her that he had requested his Jijaji who was into public dealing to help him through this and his Jijaji had agreed. He would come to Delhi when his parents were here.

"Kartik, if you don't mind, can you tell me why your eldest brother is so conservative?" she asked.

"He has three daughters, the eldest is of marriageable age now. His opinion is that my marrying a girl from a different caste will mar her marriage prospects; it will also have a negative impact on the mindsets of all the children in the family. Further, marrying you will not fetch me any dowry, while as an assistant, I can get at least eleven lakhs as dowry, part of which could be used later for paying the dowry for his daughters," explained Kartik.

"How did you counter his arguments?" she asked.

"I told him that if one member of the family goes for an inter-caste marriage, that does not automatically imply that the rest will follow suit. Although I agree that if anyone from the family decides to tread a similar path tomorrow, they will definitely draw parallels, but then they will be educated adults by that time and would be entitled to their opinions. As far as dowry is concerned, I told him that in an arranged marriage, I would get a lump sum dowry of eleven lakh as a one-time measure, which would be spent immediately. However, in this case, I will get a monthly dowry in the form of your salary cheque which will be spent judiciously for my household. And in approximately seven years from now, I will get an equivalent dowry with interest."

"Good Lord, that is a remarkable piece of calculation. So, was your brother convinced?"

"No, because he has found matches for me: one is a probationary officer in a bank and another is an MCA, both from our caste. Their parents are willing to pay that much of dowry for them. However, I feel that their fathers must either be corrupt and that is how they have accumulated so much of wealth, or they are not sure of their daughters and that is why they are willing to pay so much. Additionally, I am totally against dowry, so I said that even if they make me marry another girl from our caste, not a single rupee will come into my house from dowry.

"However, he is still after me as if I have committed a grave error, while he is not saying a thing to Jai Bhaiya, my third brother, to hurry the process of finalizing his bride-to-be. He has clearly told me that he will kill me if I even think of marrying you."

He sat down on one of the benches in the market. She held his hand and sat down with him.

"Don't worry Kartik, you have put in as much effort as a man possibly can, and I am sure nothing can go wrong with us. I will not let anything happen to you," she promised.

They had a glass of juice each to cool their heads and went back to their respective homes.

Once home, Shalini was greeted by her father, who was back from his trip.

"How was your trip Papa?" she asked fondly.

"It was fine. I heard you have bought a mobile?" her father enquired.

"Yeah, here it is." She showed him the mobile and explained its features.

"Any other development?"

"No."

"How is Kartik, Shalini?" he asked.

She looked back and sat down with him again. Shalini asked if her mother had told him everything.

"Yes, she has told me a little bit. The rest, you tell me," her father said.

"He is a good guy, Papa. He has come to our house so many times, and even you have met him. He has done his honours in Mathematics and is very intelligent too. Most importantly, he is a self-made man, just like you." She tried to highlight his degree in Maths as she was aware of her father's fondness for the subject.

Her father told her to call him home the coming Sunday at around eleven. Shalini hugged her father and assured him that he would like Kartik.

Shalini informed Kartik about her conversation with her father. He requested her to first get the horoscopes matched so that everyone could be convinced in one go.

"My father's decision is not based on matching horoscopes. My mother is already convinced about you. Having said that, I am not saying that we will not get the horoscope matched, but I am kind of scared now that if they do not match, then what? So that's a secondary issue now, because in my house, my father is the boss; if he is convinced, nothing else will matter," she concluded.

"Okay then, let Sunday be the judgement day," Kartik declared.

◆

Sunday was the 20th of October. Early morning at 6.00 a.m., there was a knock on the door. Shalini immediately got up to check if it was Kartik. "God, why has he come so early, I had called him at eleven."

She opened the door only to find her beloved Nanu on the other side of the door. "Welcome Nanu, what a pleasant surprise."

"What I have given is a very small surprise, my dear, in comparison to the surprise you have given all of us."

Her Nanu made himself comfortable in her room as her parents had gone out for a walk.

Shalini did not utter a word. Though he was her favourite, she never dared to argue with him about anything. They had always seemed to be so in sync that sometimes they were believed to be father and daughter.

"Who told you, Nanu?" she asked hesitantly.

"You feel that if you don't tell me, nobody else will? Your father told me about Kartik. Now, you tell me all about him."

Shalini told Nanu about Kartik's background, his hometown and about his family. Once her parents came back, she made tea for everyone. She made some poha for breakfast with her mother and Sindhi kadi for lunch. Her Nanu observed fondly that their little Shalini had become responsible.

"Yes, she has grown up and become responsible. Let's see what this chap Kartik is like," said her father, clearly anxious to meet Kartik.

Kartik arrived at exactly the time allotted to him. He greeted all the elders with, "Pranam," and touched their feet.

"It's nice to meet you, young man. Which place do you belong to exactly?" her Nanu started off immediately.

"Sir, I belong to Deoghar in Bihar."

"That means, you get down at Jasidih Railway Station to reach there?" he asked.

"Yes, but how do you know that, Sir?" asked Kartik who had clearly been bowled for a six.

"I also know that this place Deoghar is famous for one of the Jyotirlingas and is also famously known as Baidyanathdham," declared Nanu, exhibiting his knowledge about the place.

"Wow, that's wonderful, Sir. I am amazed at your knowledge. No doubt you are Shalu's favourite." Kartik suddenly realized that he had once again called her Shalu in front of everyone.

"My knowledge about all the things that I have just mentioned was due to my profession, so there is no need to be surprised. Also thanks for sharing with me the valuable piece of information that I am Shalu's favourite. Through this sentence you have actually enlightened us about two facts. Anyway, now let me learn some more facts, which I am not aware of. Like about your parents. Have they agreed to this relationship, since as far as I know, the caste differences could be a hindrance from your side?" questioned Nanu.

"Can I call you Nanu?" asked Kartik, becoming increasingly nervous now. Nanu nodded and comforted him.

"Yes Nanu, back home, my people are entrenched in the caste system, but I am sure, there is nothing that cannot be managed. I will convince everyone. Further, Shalu has been raised so well that it is impossible for anyone to say no to her," Kartik replied with conviction.

"Good, I am happy to hear that. Now tell me, did both of you know beforehand, that the other one is a Mathematics student and have you studied in her college, ARSD in Delhi University?" asked Nanu.

"No, we found out about this later," both of them said in unison. "I studied in St Columbus College in Hazaribagh," Kartik continued.

Nanu was impressed at how the couple had answered together, leaving them feeling embarrassed. "When can we meet your parents?"

"My parents are expected any time after Chhat Pooja. I will arrange a meeting then." Nanu asked Shalini's father if he wanted to ask Kartik anything.

"No, I think we have had a good interview with Kartik. However, I wish to let him be aware of certain things," said Shalini's father.

Kartik waited anxiously, hoping that this would not be some other kind of an interview.

"I am strictly against dowry. Whatever I want to do for my daughter, I shall do." Shalini's father looked at Kartik for a reaction. Kartik assured him that even he was against this evil custom.

"I do not believe in the caste system," continued her father.

"I used to believe in the caste system, but not now. However, my parents and other family members are entitled to their own opinions which I might not be able to change in general, but will try to convince them that my case is an exception," Kartik replied earnestly.

"Good. And lastly, my daughter is quite opinionated because I gave her the freedom to judge and form her own opinions about people and things. This could become a reason for conflict if at least one of you is not flexible. You know there is a famous saying that Indian husbands are quite flexible, so I hope you understand why I am telling you this," said Shalini's father, making everyone laugh.

"I agree, Uncleji, but believe me, Shalini is an intelligent girl. She is opinionated only with people she can be herself with, otherwise she is very flexible," Kartik said carefully.

"It's okay, son, you can call her Shalu," said her father and patted Kartik's back.

Before Kartik left, Shalini's mother told him that both of them had to now get their horoscopes matched from a pandit ji of his choice. Uday expressed his desire to accompany them, fearing that they could fudge the reports. The meeting was formally over and Kartik and Shalini also knew that matching horoscopes was just a formality now and would not be much of a hindrance, while Kartik waited for his parents to arrive in Delhi.

Kartik took some time out and made an effort to find a pandit ji with a good reputation. The following weekend, Kartik went to Shalini's house to pick her up for the match-making. Both Shalini and Kartik sat on her Scooty while Uday was on his bike.

On the Scooty, Shalini said, "Kartik, Uday might be feeling bad that I chose to sit with you and not him."

Kartik comforted her and said that he wouldn't mind if she chose to sit with her brother, but Shalini stayed put. Once there, she was nervous and had the tingling feeling once again. Both of them gave their horoscopes to the pandit ji. Kartik also let the pandit know that since he was not aware of his date of birth and other details, he had had it calculated on the basis of the Hindi calendar *tithi*.

Before the panditji studied their horoscopes, he asked them about their backgrounds. Kartik briefed him that Shalini was from Delhi and he belonged to Bihar.

"I would not discourage you but being from Uttar Pradesh, I know that men from Bihar and UP do not even like to pick up a glass of water on our own and expect our wives to do each and everything in the house, while these girls from Delhi are brought up in a liberal fashion. They want equal participation from their men. Hence, such a match can never work," explained the pandit ji, but when he saw no apparent change in the expressions of his clients, he continued with the analysis of Kartik's horoscope.

He asked Kartik some questions about his background to test the authenticity of the details provided. Once satisfied, he then proceeded to match the two horoscopes. After around fifteen or twenty minutes, the pandit ji raised his head and gave the verdict that this was not a good match. They had only eighteen matching points out of a total of thirty-six points. He informed them that they would not be able to live together for more than a year. As soon as they consummated their relationship, differences would start cropping up.

Uday was excited to hear this. "See, didn't I tell you he is not a good match?"

Shalini became worried but kept her calm and asked like a veteran in the field if there were any solutions to this problem. The pandit ji declared that the only solution was not to marry Kartik. He added that there was no scope of their being blessed with children from this match.

"You still wish to hear more good things from him? Please get up and let's go." Uday got angry.

Kartik stood and all of them came out after thanking the pandit ji.

"Di, please come with me," said Uday authoritatively.

Kartik sat on the Scooty and Shalini found herself facing the same dilemma again. She tried to explain that even Kartik would be as heartbroken as she was and would definitely like to discuss it. However, Uday reminded her that she had promised that if the horoscopes did not match, she would not marry Kartik.

"I stand by what I said. But right now, I am not marrying him, am only sitting with him on the back seat of my own Scooty," she said politely yet sarcastically.

Once on the back seat of the Scooty, she asked Kartik what he felt about the verdict. He said coolly that he did not believe in all that.

"But I do. I do not want any friction to be there between us. I cannot live fighting with you all through my life," she was almost sobbing.

"As it is your father has said that you are opinionated." Kartik was still cool about it.

"Kartik, I want to live with you all our lives, not for one year only. If that is the case, I will marry you, but will never ever consummate my relationship with you."

She was sobbing harder now.

"What is this stupidity? This way you will only make the pandit's verdict come true, because if we don't consummate our relationship, we will never have any children. I feel his verdict was highly biased as even before looking at the horoscopes, he had given his opinion against this marriage. So, let's go to your house first and find a solution to this problem." And he drove Shalini back home.

The three of them reached Shalini's house. Uday told the entire story to his mother, adding spice to it. She told him to stay calm and served them lunch. Shalini was still in a sombre mood.

"See that is why I never wanted to show the horoscopes to any pandit. Now, if we ignore it and go ahead with our marriage, and God forbid his predictions come true, then we will be cursing each other all our lives for not listening to him in the first place," she said.

Kartik tried explaining to her that different pandits give different verdicts about the same horoscopes so she need not take such things to heart. She thought about it and said that even if one pandit told her that it was a good match, she would not think twice about it. Kartik was surprised to hear that she wanted to go to another pandit. "Come on Shalu, what has happened to your logic?"

Suddenly her mother, who had developed a soft spot for Kartik, asked Shalini if they had the kundli software at home. Shalini nodded. Her mother asked her to match her horoscope with her father's with the software and to find out how many points they got. Shalini did as she had been asked, only to find that her parents had exactly eighteen points matching.

"Wow and she still had two intelligent, good looking and mature children who are not willing to grow up," Kartik laughed.

"Grow up Shalini; you should be happy that you have scored at least fifty percent by getting an eighteen on thity-six," he said.

All this while, Uday had been a silent spectator. He said, "Di, let's send these horoscopes to astrospeak.com. One of my friends did this and the site's predictions are really accurate."

All of them liked the idea. Since they would not be meeting the pandit ji personally, biased predictions were out of question. They immediately entered the details into the website and received a message that the result would be declared in a day's time.

Kartik went home. Shalini could not sleep that night. She was nervous. Both of them spoke to each other several times on phone that night. The next day, they were both in the office when the result was going to be mailed to them. However, as there was no internet in the office, they were completely dependent on Uday who was supposed to read out the predictions from home at around one in the afternoon.

As it was lunch time, Kartik came to Shalini's room, to be by her side when the result came out. He feared that she could have a nervous breakdown if the result was not positive. At around 1.15 p.m., Shalini called Uday and enquired about the predictions.

"Sorry Di, it's a negative one," he said and paused.

"What?" Shalini almost screamed.

"Oh, let me complete my sentence. It's a negative one for me and a positive one for you two," Uday finished.

"What?" she screamed again, this time out of happiness.

"Yes, you have got it right. They have given you twenty-nine points out of thirty-six. Other things mentioned in the report are also positive, none as misinformed as the pandit ji chosen by your Bihari Babu," he teased his sister.

"Now, what do you have to say, Uday?" Shalini asked.

"I had promised you, and I will live up to it though I am sceptical about him being a Bihari," Uday said.

Shalini told Kartik the verdict and both went out for lunch to their favourite Mysore Café to celebrate. Kartik asked Shalini if she was happy and she nodded.

"That means there should be no problems in consummating our relationship now," he replied as he pulled her leg. She blushed.

"Now you are blushing. Just try to remember the way you were telling me on the streets that I will not..."

"I apologize for behaving in such an idiotic manner, but please understand. I was so emotional and tense at that time that I felt that I was actually on the verge of losing my most precious relationship," she clarified.

"You were not emotional, my dear Shalu, but an emotional fool. Don't worry, I will still enjoy my life with my fool," Kartik joked.

"You called me a fool! I am not talking to you; go to that bank PO girl or that MCA girl now."

Shalini pretended to be angry with him.

"Come on, I was only calling you a fool in Hindi. You are my sunflower."

They were happy and relieved that day, as they knew that from one side at least it was a wholehearted yes and they could concentrate on the other side now. The battle was half won. That evening they even went to a temple to thank Lord Shiva. Shalini sometimes used to call up Dheeraj to know his progress and to help him in case he had any problems with his preparation. A few days later, Kartik told Shalini that his parents were going to arrive on the 30th of November. He added that Naveen Bhaiya was going to Bangalore for two months. Due to his good performance, he had been chosen to train Army School teachers there. Kartik decided to bring his Ma and Pitaji to his house directly. Naveen Bhaiya was leaving for Bangalore the next day. Kartik said that it would be good if she could also come to see him off at New Delhi Railway Station at noon. She, however, asked hesitantly if after the previous incident, his brother would like to meet her.

"He told you not to come to his house. How can he stop anyone from coming to the railway station? This way he will have to meet you at least once, though unwillingly. This is important for me, Shalu," Kartik requested.

Both of them reached the station in time only to see that Kartik's brother had not reached yet. Kartik called him to find out why. "Your Bhabhi was crying, that's why I got delayed. Now we are on our way but it will take us at least twenty minutes to reach," Bhaiya said.

"Bhaiya, there are hardly fifteen minutes left for the train to leave. Please hurry up." Kartik panicked.

"Don't worry, Indian trains are never on time," answered his Bhaiya casually.

However, when you want things to be delayed, they happen exactly on time. Bhaiya had just arrived in the parking lot of the New Delhi Railway Station, when the train whistled and started moving slowly. Kartik ran to the parking lot to help his brother with his luggage, while Shalini rushed towards the engine, which was thankfully near their bogie. The driver was standing at the entrance. She told him that her brother, an Army officer, had been called to Bangalore in the interest of the country. He was travelling by the same train and had just arrived in the parking lot. She requested the driver to wait for her brother.

"We don't want the train to be delayed, otherwise people like you complain that Indian trains are never on time. However, as it is for the sake of our country, I will wait for him. Just wave your hand when he gets on the train," the engine driver said and the train stopped moving.

Shalini thanked him and ran towards Bhaiya's bogie. As soon as Bhaiya got onto the train, she waived to the engine driver and the train started moving. Kartik asked her whom she had been waiving to. That was when she narrated the whole story. Kartik was clearly impressed. Bhabhi immediately called up her husband and informed him how if it had not been for Shalini, he would not have been able to catch the train that day. She told him to remember how badly he had spoken to her over phone the other day and that she had still gone out of her way to help him.

Naveen thought about it and felt guilty for his behaviour. He immediately messaged Kartik and apologized about his views on Shalini. He assured Kartik of his support. Kartik shared the news with Shalini and thanked her for her timely support.

A few days later, Kartik's parents reached Delhi. Kartik dropped them home and went to office hurriedly. He told Shalini that he would probably not be able to come to drop her in the evening as he wanted to spend time with his parents these few days. Shalini comforted him and said that it was perfectly fine.

That evening, when he reached home, Dheeraj had already informed his parents about Shalini and Kartik's relationship. Kartik sat beside them. "She is really a nice girl, Pitaji. Please meet her once."

"That's fine son, but how can I even think of your marriage when your elder brother's has not been decided yet. Further, who are these people? I do not have any clue as to who Sindhis are. Somebody told me that they are very stingy people, always fighting about petty matters. How can I get my son married into such a family?" His father explained his dilemma.

"These are all apprehensions which will vanish once you meet her parents. I am not telling you to get us married right now. I would not like to get married before Jai Bhaiya. Pitaji, please just meet them once," he pleaded.

"No, I will not meet anybody till Jai gets married," Kartik's father gave an ultimatum.

Kartik chose to keep quiet as he knew that it would be futile to say anything. He wanted to wait for his Jijaji.

At night his mother asked him if Shalini was very beautiful.

"Yes, Ma, she is even more beautiful than any of my Bhabhis. Do you want to see her picture?" he asked enthusiastically and took out a snapshot from his office bag. He had kept a snapshot of Shalini in which she was with her grandmother in a temple. He knew his mother would appreciate the fact that she took care of her elders and was religious too.

"So you keep her photograph?" Kartik's mother teased him. Without reacting, he simply gave the photograph to his mother.

"Hmm...No doubt, my son who is the most eligible bachelor in his home town has fallen for her. She is definitely very beautiful, but her nose is too big. Don't you think so, Dheeraj?" she said while showing the photograph to her youngest son.

"Ma, I have already met her. She is nice to talk to. I think there is no harm in meeting her parents once," said Dheeraj in order to help his elder brother.

"That's okay. But you know how adamant your father is," their mother remarked.

The following Sunday, Kartik's Bhabhi arrived with her kids. She pointed out how Shalini had managed to stop the train and help Bhaiya, indicating how courageous and intelligent she was.

"Delhi is the capital and people from different cities, towns and states come and settle down here. I have seen girls, even those from Bihar who, after coming to Delhi, start wearing clothes and using words that are enough to embarrass anybody. On the other hand, Shalini is humble, respectful, courteous and religious," Bhabhi said.

On Kartik's insistence, Ma showed Shalini's photograph to Pitaji. Kartik, however, was becoming increasingly disappointed and told Dheeraj that it was possible that even Jijaji might not be of any help now.

Pitaji was a man whose reasoning was very simple. He knew he always had the right and authority to say no if he did not like either the girl or her family and no one would be able to challenge his decision. However, he wanted to see his elder son settled first as per societal norms.

The next day Kartik was getting ready to go to office when he saw his father sitting alone. He went up to him, sat on the floor and told his father warmly that if he ever decided not to accept Shalini or her family, he would in no way go against him, but in such a case, he would never marry.

His father explained, "Have I ever said no to anything that you wanted to do? Being a father to so many children, I was always short of money, but your Ma and I ensured that all our children were educated. I understand your feelings, but want you to understand my dilemma too. I only want Jai to be married first."

Kartik nodded and left for office. He was convinced that his father was at least willing to meet Shalini's parents, albeit at a later stage. There was no point arguing with him.

Two days later, at around five in the evening, Kartik's Jijaji arrived in Delhi on the pretext of some official work. He called up Kartik and told him to bring Shalini to a certain restaurant so that he could have a word with her before he could persuade Kartik's parents.

Kartik and Shalini were in their respective offices. They left the office at 5.30 p.m. for Coffee Home situated in Netaji Nagar. Shalini was looking extremely simple in her blue-green khadi kurta. When Kartik introduced the two, she touched his Jijaji's feet in the restaurant. Jijaji was overwhelmed.

Jijaji was around fifteen years older than Kartik. Since it is self-service in all Coffee Homes, both men decided to pick up the coffee and a plate of idlis. Once at the counter, Jijaji asked Kartik as to how many participants had been part of the ISTM trip and was actually amused to hear that there had been twenty-five participants in all, with Shalini as the only female candidate.

"Kartik, I am sure you were not the only one vying for the attention of the only lady in the group, but seems you were definitely the one who won the contest. I personally do not find anything fascinating about you, so I wonder what caught her attention. Tell me, how did you do it?" Jijaji teased him.

"That's my charm, my hidden charm, Jijaji," said Kartik and both of them laughed.

The two of them then sat down with their coffee. Jijaji asked Shalini in a very straightforward manner why she wanted to marry Kartik.

What kind of a question is that, and what am I supposed to say. Should I say I love him, cannot live without him, because I get those tingling feelings whenever I make eye contact with him or when he touches me. Shalini thought about it for a moment, and then replied, "Because he is a good person."

"That was an intelligent answer, Shalini." Jijaji laughed.

Before leaving, she again touched Jijaji's feet. Once they were out of the café, Kartik asked Jijaji what opinion he had formed about Shalini.

"That I will let you know in the presence of your parents," Jijaji said with a smile.

J ijaji was the son-in-law of the family, and as Indian customs go, was the most important member of the family. That is why it was not easy for Pitaji to say no to him.

Once home, Jijaji was welcomed by everyone. Kartik and Dheeraj quickly made dinner for everyone. Later that night, Jijaji spoke to Pitaji about Shalini. Pitaji informed him that he had not met her or her parents and did not wish to talk about this issue till Jai got married.

"Jai, as I understand, will be getting married within the next one or two months, because he has almost finalized a match. He is only waiting for you to come back. That means once Jai gets married, you will have to come back to Delhi to meet Shalini's parents, go back to make arrangements for Kartik's marriage at home and come back again with the *baraat*. Will that not be a little hectic for you at this age?" Jijaji said tactfully.

Pitaji asked if Kartik had approached him. Jijaji denied it but confirmed that Kartik had informed him about her and from his description he felt that she was a respectful and intelligent girl. He also informed Pitaji that while he was coming to Delhi, Kartik's sister had informed him that Jai had finally said yes to a girl.

"So I thought there should not be any problem meeting her parents once, while you are still in Delhi," Jijaji explained.

"Oh! Is that so? Jai was telling me that he has finally been able to choose a girl, but I did not think that he was serious," answered Pitaji. He continued after a pause, "Then I think you are right; it would be difficult for us to commute so many times in a short span. It would be better if we meet Shalini's parents once."

"Your decisions are always right, Pitaji," Jijaji responded. Pitaji decided that they should call Shalini's parents first.

"Sure. I will ask them to come tomorrow if you insist Pitaji," said Kartik innocently; he had been listening to the conversation from outside the room.

He ran out of the house onto the terrace, where he normally went whenever he wanted to speak to Shalini.

"I have good news!" Kartik was excited.

"What?"

"Jijaji is great! He is superb, he is a superhero! I just can't tell you how happy I am, Shalu."

"Please tell me what happened. Has he convinced Pitaji?"

"Convinced is too small a word. He managed to lead the conversation and in just two lines and exactly one minute he has made them say yes to meeting your parents; it was faster than cooking a packet of Maggi." Kartik laughed his heart out.

"You seem to be very happy and relieved, Kartik," Shalini said enthusiastically.

"Yes, I am feeling very relieved now. When Pitaji was not agreeing to meet your parents, I was tense. I was feeling the unspoken pressure."

Both of them remained silent for a moment when Shalini said that even she was happy, but at the same time feeling nervous.

"It's okay, don't be nervous. My parents are very cool. Now just let me speak to your father so that I can brief him about tomorrow's meeting."

Shalini went into her parents' room, briefed her father about Kartik's call and handed over the mobile to him. Kartik informed her father about the meeting.

"I will come along with Shalini's Nanaji," replied her father.

"I wanted to make a request," Kartik added hesitantly. Her father told him to go ahead.

"If my father enquires about your caste and gotra, please tell him that you are Brahmins, and some Brahmin gotra," Kartik explained.

"How do these things matter? We are living in the 21st century and are still talking about such things." Shalini's father was clearly annoyed.

"Uncleji, my parents have lived their entire life in a rural area where such things matter a lot even today. I, therefore, request you most humbly that for our sake, do give it a thought even though it may seem like a petty issue," Kartik pleaded.

Though Shalini's father had never believed in such things, he agreed for his daughter's sake. He then spoke to his father-in-law and charted the programme for the next day.

Kartik, on the other hand, requested the elders in his house not to talk about dowry. All of them expressed their resentment at once. However, Kartik did not budge from his position and explained that he was strictly against such a demand. His Jijaji and Bhabhi tried to explain his market worth. They even tried pointing out that part of the money from the dowry could be used for his eldest brother's daughter's marriage, but nothing worked.

"I am not a saleable item, Bhabhi. I refuse to be sold. Additionally, as far as the marriage of my niece is concerned, contributing to that will be my responsibility which I will share with my wife and will fulfil it completely. But this can never be the responsibility of my in-laws. Further, I am a government servant, and am bound by certain rules which I shall never break." Kartik stuck to his point rather forcefully.

Before anyone else could say anything, his father said, "If the boy, who would keep the major chunk of the dowry himself, does not want anything, then let it be this way. We will neither demand nor discuss this with them."

The next day, before they were leaving to meet Kartik's parents, Shalini's mother requested them to be patient. While Kartik took a day off, Shalini had already left for office as she just could not handle the stress and had decided to immerse herself in work. On their way, Shalini's grandfather bought a bouquet and sweets for Kartik's parents. After exchanging pleasantries, the three men spoke to each other about their professions. After a while, Shalini's grandfather came to the point. He said that they had already met Kartik and proposed that his parents should also come and meet Shalini the coming weekend.

His father was about to nod when Jijaji interrupted, "Why wait till the weekend? I will be leaving tomorrow."

"Yes, even I would like him to come along for the *kanya nirikshan*," Kartik's father confirmed. Jijaji realized that they might not have understood the term. He explained, "It's the interview of the girl."

"Sure, then let us have the nirikshan today itself," Shalini's father suggested.

"Sure, why not. But before that, can I know your caste please?" asked Kartik's father.

"We are Sindhis," Shalini's Nanu informed them.

"So you are refugees?" Jijaji probed further.

"My father had come from Pakistan, and settled down in Uttar Pradesh. Then for some reason, the family moved to Delhi when I was around five years old only," Shalini's father explained earnestly.

"What is this, Kartik? They are Pakistanis, they are not Indians," panicked Kartik's father.

Kartik had not anticipated such a situation. He did not know how to tackle this angle now. Before he could think of an idea, Shalini's Nanu who had sensed the panic in the air, tried to explain, "We are not Pakistanis. On the contrary, we are more Indian than any of them who were Indians residing here at the time of the Partition. We wanted to be here in India, our motherland, and that is why we left our beloved and belongings, our land, our property, our shops, everything that we owned over there."

There was silence for a while after this, when suddenly Kartik remembered something and said that just like them, Sindhis even had a caste system.

"Oh...good, what is your gotra?" asked Pitaji.

"Their gotra is Bharadwaj," Kartik again chimed in, while Shalini's father looked at him.

"I agree with Kartik that I am a Brahmin, because I believe in being Brahmin by virtue of my karma, than being Brahmin by virtue of my birth," Shalini's father replied.

"And what do you mean by that?" asked Piatji.

"I mean I truly believe in Brahmanism. We don't have non-vegetarian food and, I don't do anything which is not in the interest of my family or society or anything which I may feel guilty about; I believe in doing good deeds," Shalini's father said. Nanu was puzzled and looked at his son-in-law with great admiration.

"Good to hear that you are true Brahmins. We will come today in the evening," confirmed Kartik's father who felt that Shalini's parents' ideology matched his principles.

"Since your son-in-law is leaving tomorrow, let's get the kids engaged today," Shalini's father suggested.

Kartik's father and Jijaji looked at each other as they could not understand what 'getting engaged' was. Bhabhi, who had been in Delhi for a long time now, was aware of this concept so she chimed in; everyone agreed.

"Mind blowing! What a conversation!" Kartik thought.

When Shalini's parents left, he went out and called Shalini immediately and informed her that they were going to be engaged that very day. Shalini was shocked to hear that.

"Shalu, my dear Shalu, I am serious. In fact, I am seriously excited."

"But I am not. I cannot, I mean, I am not prepared to get married today."

"You idiot, we are not getting married today; we are only getting engaged. I was very happy and thought you would be even happier; but you seem rather indifferent." Kartik was surprised.

"No, please don't get me wrong. I am happy. Very happy. But I am surprised at this sudden turn of events. I was not expecting this. Can you please tell me how they reached this decision all of a sudden?"

Kartik comforted her and narrated the events.

"I have understood everything and am feeling better. Let me discuss this with my family and I will get back to you," she said and disconnected the call.

As soon as she kept the phone down, she got a call from her mother who told her to come back with Kartik. She said it was urgent as they had to go shopping for the engagement ring. Shalini did as she was directed.

Before Kartik could leave, Bhabhi and Ma told him to buy a sari, ring and a make-up kit of Shalini's choice for her as her gift. Shalini and Kartik reached Shalini's house from where they were to leave for Karol Bagh market. They had just stepped out of the house when it started raining.

Despite the shower, they went out on the Scooty, enjoyed themselves in the rain and shopped, after which both of them left for their respective houses.

In the evening, Kartik came over with his family, while Shalini's family prepared to welcome the guests. When they arrived, everyone touched Kartik's parents' feet. After some time, Shalini was taken to the drawing room. She was wearing a blue sari with very light make-up. Kartik, who was in his usual t-shirt and jeans, was mesmerized when he saw her in a sari for the first time. His mother called Shalini to sit with her.

Shalini's brother got the rings when suddenly, Kartik's father announced that he wanted to ask Shalini a few questions. Everybody froze.

There was pin drop silence when Pitaji asked his first question. "I know, you are highly educated, so I will not ask you anything related to your education. However, I want to test your practical knowledge, since that is what you need the most after marriage. Tell me since both of you are working, who will look after your children?"

Not expecting such a question, Shalini tried to figure out whether in such a situation she should feel shy, as was often seen in Hindi movies or whether she should actually find a way out. She decided to follow her heart and be truthful while replying. "Pitaji, I think that more than the love and care of the parents, it's the love and undivided attention of the grandparents that the children yearn for. Even my parents are working, and my brother and I have got so much of love, care and attention from my grannies that I don't remember for how long I believed that my Dadiji was my mother."

Kartik's mother was very impressed by the answer, so she asked the next question, "I have seen a photograph of yours in which you were wearing jeans, but I must tell you that such attire is strictly not allowed in villages. A daughter-in-law has to be in a sari all the time."

"Why not, Ma? I believe in, '*Jaisa desh, waisa bhesh,*'" said Shalini immediately.

"Good, tell me how will you make *khichdi pulao*?" asked Pitaji.

Shalini thought, we make either khichdi or pulao, what must be khichdi pulao? This one is tricky. Shalini decided that it was time to admit that she had heard this term for the first time. Pitaji, who by profession was a teacher, liked explaining things. He explained the recipe, which everyone listened to carefully.

After this, he asked two more questions. When he was satisfied, he indicated that they should carry on with the ceremony. Shalini was relieved that the interview was finally over and that she must have scored approximately ninety percent.

Shalini and Kartik exchanged rings amidst applause. Gifts were exchanged after this. While giving the make-up kit to Shalini, Kartik's Bhabhi whispered in Shalini's ears, "This kit is only a formality. Kartik likes you sans make-up, and he had specially told me to mention this to you." Shalini smiled.

The next day, during their lunch meet, Kartik said, "You looked amazingly beautiful yesterday."

"Really?" she asked.

"You don't believe me?" Kartik was surprised to hear this.

"How can I believe you Kartik? On the one hand you tell me that you like me without make-up, and then you appreciate me when I am wearing make-up," she complained.

"Oh! So you were wearing make-up yesterday? I never knew that. It clearly means that make-up or no make-up, I like you anyway." Kartik tried to make-up for his ignorance.

"But why were you dressed in casuals?" she asked.

"Because this is the way I am. Further, I never knew the importance of this ceremony. I was actually not aware that you would be wearing a sari. We never even discussed our outfits. Had I known this, I would have worn something so I could look at least half as enchanting as you," he said lovingly.

They looked at the rings on their fingers. Now they were least bothered about what the others would think of them as they had the licence to be together.

"My parents were highly appreciative of your answers and said that your practical knowledge is far better than mine. Pitaji also appreciated Uday a lot. To him, Uday looked like someone who belongs to the Nehru khandan. He had certain inhibitions about a Sindhi family and all those have now been put to rest," said Kartik.

"Now, what is the next step?" Shalini asked.

"My parents will be going back to Deoghar to get Jai Bhaiya married off and then it will be our turn. Should I tell you what we will do after that, or should I stop here?" he asked mischievously.

"No it's okay, you can stop here."

"Why? Do you already know what we will do after that?" he probed further.

"Kartik, please let us go back to office, we are getting late," Shalini tried to change the topic.

"But, why do you change the topic every time. I worry whether you will allow me to talk about this even after we get married," Kartik teased her.

"Hmm..." Shalini kept quiet.

"No, your silence will not work this time. You have to give me an answer. My future is at stake," he said feigning innocence.

Hearing this, Shalini just could not stop laughing and said, "Come on now, don't tell me you will only be talking even after we get married." Both of them laughed their hearts out at this.

A few days later, Kartik's parents left for Deoghar. Jai's marriage was finally fixed for the 6th of January. They had to be home by the 31st of December. Kartik gave Shalini the good news. He added that except Dheeraj, all of them would leave for the wedding on 31st December itself.

"Dheeraj has an exam on the 4th of January, so he will be leaving the next day."

It was the 30th of December, 2003, a working day. Kartik was to leave the following day. Both Kartik and Shalini had taken half the day off to spend some time together at their Sarojini Nagar quarter that day.

Once in the house, they took a round of the whole place. It was a small type-3 house and had two rooms with a veranda and a lawn.

"Tell me some good things about this house Kartik," Shalini said suddenly.

"Number one, it's so close to the Sarojini Nagar market that we can walk down to the most popular market in Delhi. Number two, I can live with you in this house – a life together for which we have made such an effort.

Number three, we, with our collective effort can have so many, many, many children here," was Kartik's impromptu reply and then he hugged her.

He then asked, "Tell me, do you agree with point one?" She nodded.

"Do you agree with point two?"

"Definitely yes."

"And what about point three?" he winked at her.

"I think we should discuss it once we are married and not now," she said.

"I don't think so. In fact, you should learn something from your friend Raavi. See the level of her commitment to Mohak that she was living with him even before marriage," he said mischievously.

"I never said that and even if that was the case, it was only after their court marriage."

"I don't believe in court marriages, hence for me that marriage is null and void. So as I see it, she was living with him day and night even when she was not married to him."

"Kartik, we will have only two children, I think that should clarify point three and that brings an end to this topic." Shalini was not allowing him a free hand.

"Okay, but what about the effort towards this goal?"

"After we get married."

"Good, I will wait till then."

He pretended to not like the idea much, though.

"You don't have a choice, Mr Vats," she said firmly.

"Okay, as of now, I just hope everything goes well there and in accordance with our plan." He suddenly became serious and changed the topic.

She sat down on the floor and said, "I hope so, too. Kartik, I will miss you. Since we have been together, this is the second time that you will be going for such a long period. You will get busy with your relatives and various ceremonies and here I will...." Before she could complete her sentence, she had tears in her eyes.

"Oh! Please don't cry. I am not going forever. I will come back in fifteen days. And what do you think? I won't miss you there? In fact, I become lonely amongst my own people and the irony is that I can't even share my feelings with anyone around me. Right now, I was feeling happy that this would probably be my last visit home without you. The next time I will be going there with my wife – Mrs Shalini Vats." He sat down too, holding her arm while she kept her head on his shoulder.

"This sounds different from Shalini Pahilajani."

"Not only different, but sounds better too," he said.

"No comments," she said and laughed.

"Oh! So you just want to be politically correct?" he teased.

"Maybe, but one thing I am sure of is that I will miss you more than you will miss me."

"You cannot say that, else I will say that I will miss you N times more," he said to cheer her.

"I will miss you an infinite number of times, maybe even beyond infinity," she replied.

"Okay, let's not fight like typical Maths students," he said and both of them got ready to leave.

"Kartik, I will wait for you. Please come back soon." Shalini hugged him.

"I sure will and please don't get emotional. I love your inner strength and will always choose a strong and brave Shalini over an emotional one. So, just chill." He kissed her forehead.

The next day, Kartik left for his village in Deoghar. Shalini's father called up Kartik to congratulate him on his brother's marriage. Kartik apologized for not having invited them for the marriage. As he was a younger brother, for his relatives, he could not have got engaged before him. Shalini's father comforted him and said that he understood these things.

The next day, Shalini was in her office when Sunaina came in and noticed the ring on her finger. Shalini tried to hide it, but Sunaina took her hand and congratulated her.

"Shalini, where is the Most Wanted Man? I did not see him around," she enquired.

Shalini blushed and informed Sunaina about Kartik's brother's wedding. Sunaina assumed that the wedding bells for them too were just round the corner.

"Maybe."

"But, how did his parents agree to an inter-caste marriage?"

So, Shalini narrated the entire story to her and Sunaina wished her all the best.

Later she called Dheeraj to check how well the preparations were going.

"Yeah, Bhabhi, but I wish I was in Deoghar to attend the marriage," he replied innocently.

"That you definitely must be, but this crucial time will not come back. So, study hard and make us proud."

"Sure, and thanks for this valuable advice. Now I will be able to concentrate better."

On the day of exam, Shalini called up Dheeraj and wished him well and took an update after the exam as well. Dheeraj was overwhelmed by Shalini's concern.

The next morning, on the 5th of January, Shalini was getting ready when her mobile rang. It was Dheeraj.

"Bhabhi, I wanted to tell you something," Dheeraj's voice indicated sudden panic.

"What happened, Dheeraj? Is there any problem?" she panicked even more.

"Bhabhi, Jai Bhaiya is not traceable. There is a lot of chaos at home. Everyone is worried. They have told me not to come, but I am going," he said, sounding hysterical.

Shalini immediately called Kartik to find out the problem, but there was no response. She tried around five or six times but he would not answer the phone. So, she called Dheeraj back and asked him to explain everything.

"Bhabhi, I have got another call and now it seems even Kartik Bhaiya is not traceable," he said.

"What?" She was shocked and thought that was probably the reason why Kartik was not picking up the phone.

"They have told me strictly not to come over. I don't know what to do, but I cannot just keep waiting here for more bad news," he said, almost crying.

"What time is your train?" She tried to maintain her composure.

"At 7.00 a.m. I am leaving for the station now."

"Okay! Just be calm, keep me informed. I am also coming to the station."

Shalini informed her mother that she was going to New Delhi Railway Station to see Dheeraj off and give him a few namkeen packets for the journey and would go to office directly from there.

She planned not to reveal anything to her parents as it was possible they would feel disturbed. She dressed quickly, took the keys of her Scooty and went out. However, as fate would have it, the Scooty just would not start. She tried kick-starting the Scooty, but to no avail. As there was not much time left, she quickly thought of taking an auto to the station and informed her mother of the change in plan. She was in the auto when she got another call from Dheeraj.

"Bhabhi, they've been kidnapped!" Dheeraj cried.

"What? What for? I mean, why have they been kidnapped?" she asked almost shouting, while the auto rickshaw driver also looked behind on hearing the term 'kidnap'.

"That's a long story. I can't explain it on the phone."

"Where have they been taken?"

"Munger."

"How much have they asked for?"

"They don't want money, it's something else," he hesitated as he said this.

"Okay! Just don't board the train. I am coming," she said hurriedly as she tried to figure out the reason for their kidnapping.

When she reached the station, the train was just about to leave. Dheeraj was standing at the entrance of one of the bogies.

"Get down with your bag Dheeraj," Shalini almost screamed as the train began to move.

"But I want to go," he screamed back.

"Do you want to help them or not?"

"Yes."

"Then do as I say; get down immediately."

He got down. Shalini asked him to tell her exactly what had happened.

"Whatever has happened is so shameful that I am unable to understand how to tell you."

"Please tell me, whatever it is, and keep in mind that we don't have much time."

"Jai Bhaiya had refused many girls, some on account of looks and yet others for dowry. One of them was a proposal from Munger, from a village called Kalai. They were poor people and could not afford the dowry Jai Bhaiya had asked for. The girl's brother, who was a small time goon, got to know that Jai Bhaiya was getting married to someone else. Clearly annoyed with the development, he and some of his associates tried to kidnap Jai Bhaiya. Kartik Bhaiya, who happened to be there with him at that time, tried to intervene, but both have been kidnapped and are being held captive in their village."

"Now what will they do with them?" Shalini asked, clearly worried for both of them.

"Generally, in such cases, the kidnapped guy is forcibly married to the girl. This is called zabaria shaadi. My parents are worried about Kartik Bhaiya too as the girl in question has a younger sister," Dheeraj explained.

Shalini, who had been standing in front of Dheeraj until then, sat on the ground. She just could not believe her ears.

"What am I supposed to do now?" she thought. Dheeraj helped her to get up and made her sit on the bench.

"It's a blackout for me. I don't know what to do." She felt like crying but even tears failed her. Everything seemed to be going so wrong. She was tense and there were knots in her stomach.

"Dheeraj, I am not sure whether what I am thinking is correct or not, but I will have to try."

She mustered up her courage and gave him money to buy two tickets for Munger. She went to her office to make other arrangements.

No wonder Bhaiya told me that she is very courageous, thought Dheeraj.

Once in office, Shalini went straight to Sunaina's room, brought her out and narrated the whole story.

"So, now you are planning to go to Bihar?" asked Sunaina. Shalini nodded.

"Are you mad? You think you are some filmi hero that you will go there, talk to those goons and they will leave Kartik and Jai?"

"I know that this will not be that easy. But I just can't wait for Kartik to come back with somebody else as his wife," responded Shalini.

"Shalini, please try to understand, they are not good men. You are a girl, and any untoward incident could take place."

"Ma'am, I had come to you as you had offered me help. When I came to know of this incident, I could not think of anybody else but you. You are my only friend in this office and in whom I have always confided. Please help me," Shalini pleaded with Sunaina.

Sunaina thought for a moment and said, "Okay! I will speak to my brother who is an SP in Deoghar and will ask him what can be done in such a case."

Both of them then went to their respective rooms. Shalini called Dheeraj and he confirmed that he had got the tickets.

Later Sunaina gave Shalini her brother Akhilesh Prasad's mobile number. "When you reach Sultanganj Railway Station, just give him a call and coordinate with him," instructed Sunaina. Shalini thanked her friend and left. Sunaina wished her the best and hoped to see the couple together soon. She applied for leave for Shalini.

Shalini was on her way to the station when she called up Kartik, but the call would just not go through. She then called up Uday and told him everything.

"Are you mad, Di?" he was furious on hearing her plan to leave for Bihar.

"No, I am in my senses," she replied in short.

"No, you are not, those people will kill you."

"I am going under full protection, Uday. I told you, the SP of Deoghar will help us."

"Di, the most harm that could come to Kartik is that he might be married to another girl."

"No, he could be killed if there is no police intervention."

"How! They wanted one groom, now they are getting two so that's actually a bonus. Why would they kill him?"

"If the potential groom is not willing to marry, then he may have to pay with his life."

"Do you know what harm could befall you?" he asked.

"Yes, but when I am under full police protection, no one can dare to touch me."

"Okay! Then I am also coming with you."

He was about to disconnect the call when Shalini said, "No, wait. Listen to me carefully; you cannot leave Mummy and Papa in the lurch. If something happens to me, at least you will be there with them. I have Dheeraj with me. He is like a younger brother, obviously not as good as my own brother, but I have faith in him so please stay there," she pleaded.

"Di, have you informed Mummy and Papa?" Uday asked.

"No and I leave it to your sensibilities about how you want to tackle the situation. I will keep you informed of all my moves," she said and disconnected the call.

The train was already on the platform when she reached. They settled down in their berths.

Dheeraj saluted her for her courage and hoped that their efforts would not be in vain and that they were able to help his brothers out of this mess. Shalini assured him that together they would definitely pull the two brothers out of it.

After that, there was silence between them. Dheeraj, as the youngest in the family was used to his elders' instructions. But this time, Shalini, an outsider, was giving the instructions and he was not quite sure of what he was doing. He, however, knew that whatever she was doing was not only in the interest of his brothers, but in the interest of the entire family.

On the other hand, Shalini was thinking hard as well. Where am I going? What am I doing? Am I truly as safe as I made Uday believe I was? God, please help me. I believe in you, I have never done any wrong to anybody, at least knowingly. Please help Kartik, give those goons some wisdom.

Dheeraj asked Shalini if she wanted some tea when the tea vendor came, but she refused to buy any. She took out namkeen packets for him. That was when she realized that she had not got anything for herself – no bag, nothing at all.

How will I be able to survive? On second thought, if I am not able to rescue Kartik, I may not be able to survive in any case, so there is no point in thinking about these things, she thought and was reminded of the time when Kartik had told her that he liked a brave and courageous Shalini more than an emotional one. She hoped that her actions were in accordance with his ideas.

She was thinking of Kartik, his mischievous ways, his leadership qualities; she realized that she had never been able to say or even hear those three magical words from him.

What the hell? Will I ever be able to tell him how much I love him, that I am not even able to think of a life without him, that I want to grow old with him, that he is the best man I have ever met and how I wish to be called Shalini Vats.

The next day, Shalini and Dheeraj were up early as they had to reach Sultanganj Railway Station by 11.30 a.m. It was Shalini's first journey in a train bound for Bihar. People in the bogie were discussing the change in leadership they were expecting after the impending elections in Bihar. There was a lot of commotion in the train. People were divided into two groups and were discussing the lives of the leaders like Nehru and Shastri, one after another like they were veterans. While one group was sure that Shri Lal Bahadur Shastri had a heart attack, the other was more than certain that Shastriji had been poisoned at Tashkent, and had not died from natural causes. Both were giving reasons to support their claim. The next leader to be discussed was the freedom fighter Netaji Subash Chandra Bose. It seemed to Shalini that people from Bihar, irrespective of their age, were deeply interested in Indian politics.

"No doubt this is why Kartik used to tell me that politics is in the veins of Biharis, whether young or old, literate or illiterate."

How she liked being a part of such discussions. On any other occasion, she would have actually jumped into the conversation, but that day she kept herself aloof. Later, people around her were buying *litthi-chokha, jhal moori,* etc. She almost felt deja vu when she heard the voice of a vendor at the Jamalpur Station *'har ek station se kharab chai'*. She remembered how Kartik had explained how good this marketing tactic works for him and fetches him a lot of buyers. He had wanted to take her along to Bihar the next time he went, and had described how they'd enjoy the journey having jhal moori together. She requested Dheeraj to buy some jhal moori for her.

Tears fell from her eyes for the first time when she took the first bite. She felt like bursting into tears like a child, but knew that Dheeraj was very vulnerable too and that she could not break down in front of him. They were about to reach Sultanganj Station when she called SP Akhilesh Prasad, Sunaina's brother.

He confirmed that his sister had told him everything. He comforted Shalini and told her that the SP of Munger had assured full co-operation and had sent a team of around ten policemen. They would meet them at Tarapur.

Once they got down at the station, Shalini tried calling Kartik once again. Fortunately this time, he picked up the phone.

"Shalu, my dear Shalu, thank God that you have called. I was, in fact, about to call you." His voice sounded tired.

While keeping her emotions in check, she asked his exact location hastily and informed him that she would be reaching there in no time with a police team."

Kartik was surprised to hear this and told her that they were being held in a small room in the backyard of a house belonging to someone called Badrinath Thakur.

"Both of us had been tied up here, initially. However, they have taken Jai Bhaiya with them just now to marry him to their sister. They were planning to take me too, but I told them that if they even think of doing such a thing to me, they will be jailed because I am a central government employee, and that I will never accept such a marriage and would leave their sister right there. So they have gone out to discuss my case," he replied.

"How far is this place from Tarapur?" she asked.

"About eight kilometres," he replied.

Shalini requested him to just keep them busy for an hour or so, till she arrived with the police.

"Quickly Dheeraj, let us please take a cab, auto or whatever public transport we can get; we need to reach Tarapur as soon as possible," Shalini requested.

"A taxi will cost a lot." Dheeraj was sceptical. She pointed out that if they weren't quick, the goons would make them pay even more.

Dheeraj asked if she had had a word with Kartik Bhaiya. She said yes and told him excitedly about the discussion while they got into the taxi.

It took them half an hour to reach Tarapur. It was a big, crowded market place where it was difficult to trace the exact location of the police. Shalini observed that she was at the receiving end of lots of stares from passers-by. Dheeraj noticed and could see the discomfort on her face. He came and stood near her and told her that she was wearing jeans and a top which was why she was being stared at. "Girls here are either in suits or saris with their heads properly covered." Shalini remembered what Kartik's mother had told her.

Time was running out and Shalini's patience too. She repeatedly called up SP Munger to find out where his men were. After about half an hour, she got a call from his policemen who said that they were about to reach Tarapur. She gave them her exact location.

"My BP will shoot up now if they don't turn up in five minutes," she told Dheeraj.

"Why can't we go there on our own? We would reach even before the police," he said.

"And, what will we do there? How will we tackle those goons? We will not be able to handle the situation without the police, but I agree that we should not be waiting here any longer."

She told Dheeraj to look for a vehicle which could take them directly to Kalai. They were about to hop into an auto when they heard a loud horn from a gypsy. It was the police. They got into the gypsy and the vehicle zoomed towards its destination. The team was led by Sub-Inspector Gupta. Shalini narrated the story to him. He told her that many such incidents had occured in the past, however, these days it was not very common.

"If a zabaria shaadi is taking place, it means that somebody from your family has divulged the details to them. The miscreant is amongst you only."

Both Dheeraj and Shalini looked at each other in disbelief.

"No Sir, this is not possible," Dheeraj insisted.

"That we will get to know once we reach," said SI Gupta.

When they reached there, they saw that a mandap had already been set up, and Kartik was being taken to it. He was surrounded by six men, one of whom had a pistol.

The police immediately sprang into action and took control of the situation. Shalini got down from the gypsy and walked towards Kartik who was not even able to stand properly. She could see that he had been beaten black and blue, had bruises on his face, his shirt almost torn and blood was flowing down his arms. She had tears in her eyes.

He told her that Jai Bhaiya had already been married. Since Kartik had resisted, they had beaten him. "I knew you would be coming, so I was just buying time."

"By getting beaten?" she asked.

"A girl who has never lived without her parents, who till some time back was scared to be a part of an all-boys group, has come all the way to Bihar. It's commendable. You reached on time, otherwise someone else would have been Mrs Kartik Vats." He smiled at her.

"You are in so much pain, such jokes do not suit you. And some other Mrs Kartik Vats would never have been possible," she said confidently.

"Shalini, did I ever tell you how much I love you?"

"No, never. But as they say, better late than never."

Before he could say anything, SI Gupta came out with the brother of the bride and informed everyone that as he had thought, the miscreant was from their family. The culprits had confessed that they had contacted the eldest Vats brother, Pawan Vats, who had told them that if they wanted to kidnap Jai, they would have to take Kartik too, as Kartik wanted to marry some refugee. The miscreants had paid five lakhs to Pawan for both the brothers.

All four of them – Jai, Kartik, Shalini and Dheeraj – were shocked to hear this. Suddenly they could see two of Kartik's elder brothers and his Jijaji coming towards them. Dheeraj had told them everything.

As they came closer, Jai, who was clearly disappointed, shouted at Pawan, "If you had a problem with Kartik's decision, why was I made a scapegoat?"

"Jai Bhaiya, I apologize if you do not like what I am saying, but tell me what is the problem with the girl you have married.

She is beautiful, more educated than you. Then why did you reject her?" Kartik said.

"Because they were not able to..." but Jai couldn't complete his sentence as the police were present. But that did not stop Kartik who continued, "As they were not giving you the dowry you expected. If she starts working, she will earn more than you. Further, why do you want to be sold? If the youngsters do not change the old and hypocritical methods, then how will Bihar ever grow?"

Pawan reacted strongly to this and was about to slap Kartik, when Kartik added, "Bhaiya, he has already confessed that you were their informant and sold both of us for five lakhs. Now, there is no point in reacting like this."

"I didn't do this for myself. You are talking of today's youth changing Bihar. How will it change if you don't take dowry? I will still have to pay it for my daughters," said Pawan, showing no sign of remorse.

"Don't worry about her; she is as much ours as she is yours. Had I been in your place I would have concentrated more on her studies rather than her marriage. Anyway, we will discuss this once we reach home." Kartik thanked SI Gupta for his support.

Shalini thanked SI Gupta for his co-operation as well. They were about to leave when Kartik went inside to bring out his new Bhabhi.

"Don't do that, because in no way will I accept this zabaria shaadi," said Jai.

"Bhaiya, you may or may not accept it, but the fact remains that you have been married to her. It is of no use crying over spilt milk," said Kartik.

Shalini called up Uday. He told her that he and his Father and Nanu were about to leave for Munger. She informed Uday that all was well and that she was about to go back. Shalini's father took the phone from Uday and scolded Shalini for taking such a big decision without consulting him. She apologized.

"Sir, please do not register any case," Kartik requested SI Gupta.

"Why, why not?" asked Shalini immediately.

"He is my eldest brother, Shalu. How can I take action against him?"

"Both of you could have paid with your life for such a heinous act by your so-called eldest brother. He should definitely be penalised for it. And just look at him, do you see any remorse on his face?" she argued.

"Whatever it is, I cannot send my brother to jail. And what will I tell my father? That his elder son has been arrested? This will in turn malign his image in the whole of my village," Kartik explained.

However, being impulsive by nature, Shalini asked SI Gupta about the way to pursue this case further.

"Madam, I don't think you should go ahead with this case. Even if you file an FIR, his brothers will give testimonies in his favour, setting him free," said the SI.

"No, I will stand by Bhabhi. Please tell us the way out," said Dheeraj boldly. Shalini was overwhelmed at this sudden support when everyone seemed to be against her decision. She thanked Dheeraj but requested him not to go against his family as he was too young and told him that he should concentrate on his career.

"No Bhabhi, I have seen what hell you have gone through just to be able to save Kartik Bhaiya. I have seen you controlling your tears. I completely understand how difficult it is for a Delhi girl to come to Bihar for the first time in such precarious circumstances with the kind of reputation this place has. When you can do all this for the sake of my brother, who might not be acknowledging it right now, then why can't I support you?" Dheeraj requested SI Gupta to explain the procedure.

Gupta explained them that they would have to file an FIR.

"Can I file the case in Delhi?" she asked.

"Yes, because you are engaged to Kartik, it will become a marital discord case. In that case, Pawan will have to travel to Delhi every time he is summoned by the court," he explained.

"So be it," she said.

Kartik and his elders scolded Dheeraj and Kartik pleaded with Shalu to reconsider as it was a family matter and would have repercussions.

"Kartik, if your brother seemed even the slightest bit sorry, then I would not have gone ahead with this, but he has committed a crime for which he is not even feeling guilty. So, please don't tell me to do something that my heart is not ready to accept. On the contrary, you should convince your brother to accept that he is wrong."

Kartik looked at his elder brother, who as Shalini had correctly pointed out was far from remorseful.

"Shalini if you don't back out, I may have to back out from my commitment to you. I can never go against my family," Kartik said without looking at her directly. Although Shalini was stunned at his statement, she still gathered the courage to say, "I know you are tense, but once you think about it calmly, you will realize that I am not wrong."

All this while, Pawan looked satisfied. Kartik told his brother that although he would not stay in a relationship with her if she went to court, that did not mean that he approved of his actions. "Please for my sake, Bhaiya, at least admit that you have done wrong."

However, his brother did not budge from his position. Without uttering another word, Kartik immediately went back to his village with his elders. Shalini also returned to Delhi with the help of SI Gupta and his team and immediately filed an FIR with the local police station.

Shalini re-joined office and went to meet Sunaina. Shalini narrated what had happened. Sunaina said that although she agreed with Shalini's stand, she wanted to know if she was aware that this battle of hers could bring an end to their relationship.

"That will never happen, Ma'am. I am sure of him. He may be a bit angry, but will definitely come back to me."

"That's confidence! I hope it happens that way," prayed Sunaina.

Although Shalini appeared confident, she knew Sunaina ji might not be wrong. She had been trying to call Kartik since the day she had reached Delhi, but Kartik hadn't picked up her call.

A few days later, Kartik re-joined office, but did not come to meet her. When she went to his section, he pretended to be busy. She felt that she needed to give him time and space. Two days later, she got a call from Dheeraj. He informed her that Kartik had not spoken to any of his family members since they had returned and that Dheeraj too has been forbidden to speak with her; but Dheeraj had insisted on keeping her informed of the developments.

This shattered Shalini completely. "How can he part ways with me like this? He knows that I love him so much; how can I live without him? What will happen to our dream house?"

Shalini stopped going out of her section. She became quiet. She immersed herself in her files. Even during lunch, she remained glued to her seat. While going back home, she would stare at the point at Rail Bhawan where her beloved would wait for her.

They worked in the same organization and same building, too, so meeting by chance was inevitable. Whenever Kartik saw Shalini coming his way, he would change his path. However, whenever she saw him coming her way, a ray of hope would be rekindled in her heart and every time her hope turned out to be false, her heart would bleed.

One day, Shyamal came to Kartik's room and asked him the reason for not meeting him. He noticed that Kartik had lost a lot of weight.

"Nothing, nothing at all. I am fine, was just busy with office work," Kartik replied.

"Kartik, I have heard that you have broken up with Shalini. See, didn't I tell you that Delhi girls cannot be trusted?"

"No, you cannot say that. I am at fault. She is doing what she thinks is right." Then Kartik vented his tale of agony to his friend.

"Kartik, I must say, she is a braveheart. Neither of you are at fault. But without each other, both of you will remain unhappy. I, in fact, had come here to discuss my problem. My sister married an assistant from Bihar working in a ministry here. We paid a whopping dowry of fifteen lakhs to him. He has tortured her, both physically and mentally. So much so that she has come to us and is refusing to go back. Had it been possible, I would have put that cheat behind bars. Now, we have filed a case against him. My father, brother and I had taken loans in our individual capacities to meet the expenditure, and yet I am a witness to the hell that she is going through," Shyamal said and sobbed quietly.

"My sympathies are with you, but let me point this out to you that until now you had been saying that I should not trust a Delhi girl. In this case, it is a Bihari boy who has cheated a Bihari girl, proving that the place a person belongs to can never be the criteria for judging a person. You tell your sister to write a complaint against her estranged husband and we will go and file the complaint in the Vigilance section of his office," said Kartik.

Later that day Kartik thought to himself, "Even I am cheating Shalini the way Shyamal's sister has been cheated by her husband; the only difference is we are not married yet. Thinking about it, had we been married, would I have left her like this?" He felt sandwiched between the age-old traditions and his own liberated opinions.

The next day, while coming back with Shyamal after submitting a written complaint against Shyamal's brother-in-law, Kartik saw Shalini going to the canteen with the staff from her section. From what he could hear, it appeared that they were probably going for some promotion party. He was immediately reminded how earlier it was only Shalini's chirpy voice that could be heard during such gatherings, but now she seemed to be lost. He felt like crying when he heard gossips, "Look at this, yet another case of failed office romance." Even Shyamal told him to rethink their relationship.

Two months had passed since the incident. Shalini received summons to appear before the Patiala House court. A copy of the summons was sent to Pawan Vats too.

Pawan, who was a teacher in the Kendriya Vidyalaya School Ranchi decided that if he made sure Kartik got married to somebody else, Shalini could drop the case out of frustration as she would not have any reason to fight the case. Keeping this in mind, he went to his parents with the few proposals that were pouring in for Kartik.

Kartik's father was an experienced man. He immediately guessed Pawan's intentions. "Whatever you try, as far as I know Kartik, he would prefer to stay unmarried than be married to somebody other than that girl Shalini. Are you even aware of how your brother is doing after he left for Delhi? He has not spoken to us even once since then. Dheeraj has told us that Kartik is not eating properly, has stopped going out anywhere and only speaks when Dheeraj needs some help. You were the eldest of all; you should have taken care of all of them, as after me you are the *mukhiya* of the family. I regret to tell you it is Kartik and not you who is fulfilling all the responsibilities. We all know what that girl is doing is right, yet he chose to go against her decision to save the family's reputation and to save his eldest brother from being arrested. Shame on you! Instead of helping your younger brother out of the problem you created, you are creating another one."

It was the first time that Pitaji had spoken in such a stern manner to any of his sons. This made Pawan think about whether he had truly been wrong. Nonetheless, he was convinced that Kartik's marriage was the only solution to everyone's problem. However, if Kartik was behaving in such a manner, why would he even come here to get married?

The next day when Pawan went to the school, he was told that as per the school rotation policy, it was time for him to be transferred. Without any hesitation, he immediately chose Delhi as his place of posting. This way, he thought, he would be able to persuade Kartik and would also attend to the summons received, if need be.

It was April when Shalini appeared in court. However, it was Kartik who had come from the defendant's side in place of Pawan. While both of them were standing there, Shalini noticed that Kartik did not look well. Not only had he lost weight, he appeared weak. She wanted to hug him and cheer him up. His face, which used to shine with confidence, now appeared dull. Kartik informed the court that his brother has been transferred to Delhi, and was on his way. He asked that his attendance may kindly be forgiven this time and that his brother would definitely be present during the next date. The court agreed and gave a date after the summer vacation.

Shalini followed Kartik out of the court, but Kartik did not even look behind him. She watched him get onto the bus, and simply could not come to terms with the fact that it was all over between them. She checked with Dheeraj, who informed her that Bade Bhaiya was coming with the intention of getting Kartik married to someone else. The mobile phone fell from her hand when she heard this.

She reached home heartbroken and told Uday what had happened.

"Should I drop this case, Uday? What am I getting out of this? Only agony and distress? I was hopeful that Kartik would sooner or later realize that the stand I was taking was correct. However, I am afraid that his loyalty to his family is far superior than his honesty," she said and sobbed quietly.

"Di, you are a strong girl. I believe in you. However, in a family, one has to think about other aspects as well. For example, if the eldest brother is jailed, then who will look after his wife and daughters? Who will marry those girls? What will happen to his job when he comes out of jail?"

"Maybe you are right, Uday. But this way, will he ever understand the crime he committed? Why didn't he think about his wife, daughters and parents before doing such a thing? And if he did not think about his family then, why should we think about them now?" she asked.

"If you had married him, you would have been a part of that family. Would you have taken the same stand even then?"

"Yes, but then I would have been all the more ashamed of him. However, I guess, you are right in a way when you say that it would be difficult for Kartik to make a choice in such a peculiar situation," she agreed.

Later that night, she called up Uday while he was at work to tell him that she has decided to withdraw the case.

"I hope you are not doing this just to marry Kartik, because that would be foolish," he said.

"No, I am doing this to relieve myself of this stress as I have forgiven his eldest brother, and as you rightly pointed out, for those three little girls whose future will remain in the dark if anything happens to their father. And last but not the least, for Pitaji; if anything happens to his son, he will be shattered. As far as marrying Kartik is concerned, I would best like to forgive and forget him. I guess that is the only way I can be at peace with myself," she said thoughtfully.

"You will find me standing by you, no matter what decision you take, Di," he said.

"Then, please find out how to go about withdrawing the case," she requested him. After a period of two months, she was able to sleep well that day. A few days later, Uday informed her that once the court reopened after the vacation, they could withdraw the case.

The day Pawan reached Delhi, he was shocked to see Kartik, who had lost plenty of weight. He tried to explain to Kartik that whatever he had done had been for Kartik's benefit. However, Kartik was unconvinced and told him that no good could be achieved by selling one's brothers or taking dowry. Pawan recalled what his father had told him. He understood that Kartik would never agree to marry anyone other than Shalini. More than anything else, he was now worried about Kartik's health.

He spoke to Dheeraj about Kartik, who did not hesitate in telling him how wrong he was and what a nice person Shalini was. He told him how she had managed to reach Kalai, how much the couple loved each other and how neither of them was at peace now.

Pawan did feel remorseful and opened his heart to his youngest brother for the first time. He told him that whatever he had done had only been due to his concern for his daughters.

"Bhaiya, whatever your concern, how could you sell your brothers for this? You are no better than Yudhisthir from the *Mahabharata*." He added, "Once I had heard Kartik Bhaiya explaining to Shalini how we use the dowry for the niece's marriage and Shalini immediately said that getting her married to a good guy would be the responsibility of the family and all of us would together fulfil this responsibility by all means, financially or otherwise," said Dheeraj.

Pawan was surprised to hear this but felt it was too late to bring her into the family now. "I do not think she will ever forgive me for what I did."

It was May 2004. The Lok Sabha Elections had just ended and the Congress party had come to power. One of the promises made by the Party had been to expedite the work on the Delhi Metro. To live up to this promise, work on the Metro began in full swing. Although it displeased many citizens at first because a lot of routes were diverted, roadside shops razed, roads dug up and sometimes left open, everyone was co-operating as they looked forward to the future. It was turning out to be particularly difficult for people who did not belong to the city. Pawan Vats was one of those people. He had been posted to the Bawana Road branch of KVS. He used to travel from Ber Sarai to Bawana everyday on his scooter which he had got from Ranchi. As he was new in Delhi, Kartik had told him a specific route via Patel Nagar which Pawan used to take every day. It used to take him two hours to commute one way.

When at home, Pawan would try to initiate conversation with Kartik. Kartik, however, responded only if he thought the conversation necessary, otherwise he kept to himself. As the eldest, he even tried scolding Kartik badly and coaxing him, but to no avail. He called Naveen, his younger brother to discuss a way out, but he was of the same opinion as Dheeraj, although Naveen never raised his voice against his elder brother.

Pawan knew it was that one incident which had led to all his brothers and even his father going against him. He was clearly under stress due to the impending court case against him. And although none of his brothers would leave him in the lurch, he was definitely the reason for their grief.

Pawan brought his family to Delhi for the summer vacation. His eldest daughter was in the first year of graduation, while the younger ones were still in Class X and VIII respectively. He observed that Kartik took a keen interest in their studies.

He heard Kartik telling the eldest one to work hard so that she would get such a good job that marriage proposals would come on their own, rather than her father going out groom hunting or begging for a loan. "Daughters are the reason for a family's happiness. I believe in your capabilities, you too need to have faith in yourself," said Kartik to the elder daughter.

Pawan heard Kartik crying his heart out in the bathroom many times. For the first time, he really felt that his brothers were right and that he had been wrong. Elders may not always be right; sometimes it is the young who show them the correct path. He decided that he would have to set things right and the only thing he could think of was to bring Shalini home.

"When the court reopens I will apologize in front of everyone and am ready to face the punishment. My family will not be left in the lurch even when I am not there with them," he decided.

It was the 5th of July 2004. The courts had reopened after the vacation. Pawan had sent his family back. He took Shalini's phone number from Dheeraj and decided to give her a call after reaching his school.

On the other hand, Shalini and Uday had informed their parents that they would be going to withdraw the case. That day, both took leave from their respective offices. They had already informed their advocate of their decision. Once there, the advocate showed them the application he had prepared for the withdrawal of the case. Shalini and Uday read the application, Shalini signed it and the documents were submitted. They were informed that after lunch they would be called inside for a small hearing where Shalini needed to be present so that the court was satisfied that she had not made this decision under pressure.

Shalini, as a dealing assistant, had already faced the court for official reasons, during court cases filed by employees against the department. When her turn came at around 4 o'clock, she reiterated her decision in front of the court without fear or confusion. Once the court was satisfied, the withdrawal was accepted.

After school hours, Pawan tried calling Shalini up, but she had switched off her mobile as she was in the courtroom.

They came out and thanked their advocate. Uday gauged her gloomy mood so he told her that he would take her to Shankar Road for a relief party.

"What's that?" she asked.

"Now that you are relieved of this court case, I want to give you a chaat party at Sindhi Sweets Corner on Shankar Road," he said and off they went to celebrate.

On their way, there was a traffic jam at Patel Nagar. They realized that it was an accident. Since the traffic was not moving at all, Shalini decided to check out what exactly had happened. Ten minutes later, when the traffic had just cleared, Uday got a call from Shalini.

"Uday, I am in an auto, please come to Ram Manohar Lohia Hospital. It's urgent." She gave him the number of the auto rickshaw.

Once Uday reached the hospital, he saw his sister waiting for him in the auto.

"What's the matter, who is it?" he asked clearly worried.

"It is Pawan Vats, Kartik's eldest brother. I got a call from his mobile and somebody told me that they were calling on the last dialled number which had been mine. Since I was already close to the accident site, I went to check. A car had rammed into his scooter from behind and his scooter collided with the newly-constructed metro pillar. Nobody was willing to help him. He fainted and his left leg was bleeding profusely. With the help of one bystander, I managed to get him into an auto. That traffic jam was due to this accident," Shalini clarified.

Both of them took Pawan into the hospital. They tried to arrange for a doctor for him. However, the doctors refused as it was an accident and a formal complaint needed to be filed.

"But why was your number his last dialled number?" Uday asked.

"No clue," she replied.

"Have you informed Kartik?"

"I tried calling him, but he is not picking up."

"Bastard," Uday commented immediately.

"Uday, please."

"Why not? It's all because of him and his family that my sister is suffering, and now, when we are trying to help his brother, the main culprit, he is behaving in an absurd manner," Uday almost shouted.

"Uday, informing him is a secondary issue right now. What is important is that the doctors are not attending to him, as they want the police and family members to be present."

"I will arrange for a policeman and you call up Dheeraj," he said.

Shalini informed Dheeraj about the accident, who in turn informed Kartik about it. They rushed to the hospital. Meanwhile, the police came with Uday and registered the case. Pawan, too, came to his senses and asked the police what had happened.

The police informed him about the accident and the fact that a girl had brought him here. He suddenly saw Shalini shouting at the doctor, "The police has already registered the case and I am a family member; he is my elder brother. At least now you should have a look at him."

After much persuasion, the doctor agreed to give Pawan first aid. The doctor declared that Pawan had a fractured left leg, and at least two units of blood would be required as he had lost blood from the continuous bleeding. The blood could be obtained from the in-house blood bank. Shalini told Uday to get Pawan admitted with the help of the doctor, while she arranged for the blood. Suddenly Pawan called her to him and apologized for whatever he had done. When Kartik and Dheeraj arrived, they saw Pawan crying like a child and Sahlini consoling him, "Bhaiya, please don't cry. It's okay, I understand." Shalini touched Pawan's hand while trying to console him.

"No, please don't touch me; as per our customs, a lady cannot touch her brother-in-law as they become Bhawo and Bhaisur."

"How disgusting; he is still thinking about his customs," she thought. Little did she realize that he had been calling himself her brother-in-law.

Pawan continued sobbing and said that he knew now that what he had done to them had been wrong. "You really are a nice girl. You could have left me in the middle of the road for everything that I have done to you."

"It's okay Bhaiya, whatever you did was because you were concerned about your family."

Kartik and Dheeraj, who had been listening to this conversation from a distance until now, came nearer. "Dheeraj, he needs blood, let us go and arrange for it from their blood bank," Shalini said without even looking at Kartik.

Kartik signalled to Dheeraj and Dheeraj did not move from his place. So Shalini went out all alone, while Kartik followed her.

"Shalu, I am sorry," he said.

"It's okay, Kartik. Your brother needs blood; let us concentrate on that," Shalini said. She did not stop or look at him and continued walking towards the blood bank. They got two units of blood and gave it to the doctor. While the doctors did their job, Uday and Dheeraj decided to get coffee for everyone, leaving Kartik and Shalini outside the operation theatre.

"Please forgive me, Shalu," Kartik tried initiating a conversation once again.

"No, you don't need to apologize." She sat down on a bench with her head down.

"Look at me, Shalu, please."

"Stop calling me Shalu; you have lost the right to call me by that name," she shouted.

"Shalu, I love you. Say whatever you want to, abuse me for whatever I have done, but please don't leave me," he pleaded.

Trying to regain her composure, she said, "Who am I to abuse you? Only your family has that right. But, that's okay. For your information, I have withdrawn the case so you people can make merry and go ahead with your wedding celebrations now."

Dheeraj and Uday returned in the meantime. Dheeraj clarified, "Bhabhi, you did not hear the full sentence that day. Although he had been pressurised, Kartik Bhaiya never agreed to get married. In fact, he resolved not to get married at all if it was not to you."

"Then I guess he will have to remain unmarried," Shalini said and left the place with Uday.

A few days later, one Sunday morning Kartik called up Shalini. Shalini picked up the call reluctantly.

He thanked Shalini for taking the call.

"I am not selfish. Anyway, tell me, why have you called up?" she asked wryly.

"Bade Bhaiya wants to thank you," Kartik said and paused for a moment.

"Tell him I have accepted his thanks," she said and disconnected the call.

Kartik called up again. She picked up and was about to say something when she heard his Bade Bhaiya's voice requesting her to come over to his place. Shalini refused politely. Bhaiya still insisted, but Shalini didn't change her mind.

An hour later, her father called everybody to the drawing room and told them that he was expecting some guests from office for lunch. Shalini thanked the Almighty that she had some work to do now and could keep herself busy. She helped make lunch with her mother. Half an hour later, there was a knock on their door.

When Shalini opened the gate, she found it was Kartik and his elder brother. She immediately went inside her room and sat down on her bed.

"Why have they come here? What do they want? Do they want to completely drain me emotionally? Please go away, for God's sake."

Bade Bhaiya came inside her room with Kartik and said that he wanted to thank her. He made Kartik sit with Shalini and himself took a chair in front of them.

"I wanted to tell you both that whether you believe me or not, I had decided to admit in court that I was actually at fault, that I was ready for any kind of punishment. With people like both of you around, I am sure that my family will be in safe hands. That is the reason I tried calling you up that day and your number was the last one dialled on my phone. Now, I think both of you should take time to clear all your doubts."

He went out of the room and apologized to Shalini's father for his abrupt behaviour, adding that he had understood that the couple could not live without each other, although they were not admitting that at the moment.

"I think, we should give them some time to sort out their differences," said her father.

On the other hand, Kartik was trying to persuade Shalini. However, she had decided not to lend her ear to any of his arguments or persuasions.

"Shalini, I know I handled the situation wrongly, but please at least give me one chance to explain the reasons," he pleaded.

"Why do you want to explain yourself? You could have spoken to me about your reasons earlier when I came to your section, or when I tried calling you. There is no need to explain anything now. Please go away from here."

She got up from her bed, indicating that he leave the room.

Kartik and his brother left. On the way back, his brother told him not to take things to heart.

"When you can win the heart of the only girl on a trip, competing with so many others, I am sure you can manage to win the same girl if you try again. And this time you have all my support and best wishes," he smiled at Kartik. Kartik smiled back, feeling more at ease.

After this, he made it a point to go to Shalini's section every day and wish her. Since no one in her section knew anything about the tiff in their personal lives, courtesy demanded that she wish him back too.

He would send her messages throughout the day: *Sorry, please forgive me,*or, *Please be mine.* He waited for her at Rail Bhawan in the evening every day like he used to earlier, but Shalini passed right by him. His brother grew worried for him, when he saw him making mistakes that an otherwise ever careful Kartik would never make. At times, he used to forget to lock the door while going out, while on other occasions he forgot to take any money with him while going to office, and had to borrow money from fellow passengers to buy tickets too.

It was the 2nd of August 2004. Kartik had gone to Shalini's section to wish her in the morning, when Sunaina happened to be present there. Not knowing the relationship between Shalini and Sunaina, he wished Shalini. It did not take much time for Sunaina to understand the situation.

She informed him that she had come to give Shalini good news. Now that Kartik was there, she had a piece of good news for him as well.

"What is it, Ma'am?" Kartik asked eagerly, while Shalini kept to herself.

"If the two of you want to know what the good news is, contact the canteen manager and arrange for a small treat here tomorrow at eleven," Sunaina replied.

"Ma'am, I will give you a treat in the section but I think Kartik owes a treat only to the people of his section, so he may not like to be a part of it," said Shalini.

"Why not? Sunaina Ma'am is our HR. In fact, I think everyone who performs well at his job, owes her a treat as they are the people who decide our postings and we owe our success to their farsightedness." Kartik was trying to make use of the opportunity.

"Okay guys, then we will meet in the morning tomorrow," said Sunaina and left. Kartik too took his leave and Shalini was left fuming. The next day, both of them reached the departmental canteen at around the same time to make arrangements for the treat.

"You please stay out of it. It is a party in my section, let me deal with it," said Shalini when she saw Kartik there.

"I am very much a part of it, Ma'am. I hope you remember it," he replied confidently.

"Yeah, sure I remember it."

She paused for a moment.

"In that case, you pay for the entire thing. I am leaving because I do not want to share anything with you." She left immediately.

"Why do I behave like a duffer sometimes? She is right when she says that I could have clarified the matter earlier; I should not have shunted her out of my life completely," he thought.

Nonetheless, he reached her section in time; the food was ready and the guests were also already there. Everyone wanted to know the reason for the party. Sunaina told them that she was actually surprised to see that they were throwing the party without even knowing the reason, clearly indicating the level of their curiosity. "Anyway, let's enjoy the party first, and then I will tell you the reason."

"That's not done, Ma'am," asked Kartik, eager to know.

When Sunaina saw that Shalini was not responding, she said that it seemed that only Kartik was eager to know the reason.

"No Ma'am, even I wish to know the reason," Shalini said without her usual enthusiasm.

Sunaina informed everyone proudly that Shalini had topped the ISTM exam and Kartik had stood second. Everyone congratulated them. While Shalini was surrounded and was being congratulated by the people of her section, Sunaina asked Kartik what the matter was.

"Nothing Ma'am." He grew skeptical.

"I am aware of everything Kartik, from the ISTM training to ISTM results. You inform me of the latest situation on the intercom. I am concerned about her," she whispered.

He looked at her, as if trying to verify the validity of what she was saying and once he was satisfied, he agreed to tell Sunanina about the present status of their relationship. Kartik handed over the bill to Shalini in the presence of her SO once the party was over and said that he had paid the whole bill. He asked Shalini to pay him a hundred and fifty rupees which was half of the total." Left with no choice, she had to oblige.

Kartik told Sunaina the whole story. "Well, it's her trust in you that has won," Sunaina remarked. He could not understand what she meant.

"I had warned her that filing the case in court may bring an end to her relationship. However, she was confident about you which is why she got a severe jolt when you pushed her out of your life. Keep trying, I will also try to make her understand," Sunaina remarked.

Kartik was surprised to know this. "I hate myself for doing this. But now, I will never ever let her down," he decided.

A few days later, Sunaina caught hold of Shalini in the washroom and asked her if everything was over between the two of them or if they had any future plans.

"What future plans? I have stopped planning my future, Ma'am, because the future that I had planned for myself is now unimaginable."

"Don't lose hope; you are young, intelligent and beautiful. I am sure your parents must be looking for a good match for you. Or, maybe, you can even give the CSE a try again," said Sunaina trying to test the waters.

"No, I will never get married now. Never ever. And I do not feel like studying either," Shalini repeated.

"Why, do you still love him? Or, maybe you are not able to forget him. Or maybe he is still in your system and you are not able to get him out of it," said Sunaina, coming to the point slowly yet steadily.

"No Ma'am, I don't even like this word 'love' now and I really do not wish to discuss it any further."

Shalini tried to leave, but Sunaina held her by the arm and said, "Shalini just think about it; the two of you do love each other. He was definitely at fault when he stopped talking to you without giving any reasons, but now, by not giving him even one chance to make amends, you are repeating the same mistake. Allow him to say whatever he wants. If you find it convincing, go with him; or else opt out of the relationship and then throw away this ring which you are wearing even when you say that you do not believe in love."

While going home from office that day, Shalini's mind was preoccupied by Sunaina's words.

On the 23rd of August 2004, Sunaina came to Shalini's room during lunch, and asked her if she was still in possession of the government accommodation in Sarojini Nagar. Shalini nodded but said that she had planned to surrender it. Sunaina responded that she just wanted to have a look at it as she, too, wished to apply for quarters there. Shalini took her to it.

Once inside the house, Sunaina went to see each and every room with Shalini, triggering Shalini's memories of her recent past. She had not visited the house for a long time now. Suddenly, Shalini started crying. Sunaina understood but asked her what the matter was. Shalini told her friend how she and Kartik used to come there sometimes, and how they had promised to be a part of each other's lives for life. "And see how life has ended for me," said Shalini regaining her composure.

"No dear, life has not ended, it has just begun." Sunaina had just finished her sentence when Kartik entered the room.

"The stage is all yours Kartik, don't let this opportunity go this time." Then Sunaina excused herself.

"Shalini, before you say anything else, I wish to tell you that my eldest brother is twenty years older than I am. There was a time when my sister was ready to be married and Jijaji's parents were asking a huge amount as dowry. My father had a major health issue due to which he was out of work for six months. Bade Bhaiya sold his house and gave away all his wife's jewellery to meet the expenses. He even had to take a loan. Later on, when Naveen Bhaiya got a job, he vowed to pay off the rest of the loan and is still left with some of it. This is the only reason he behaved the way he did. He is a kind of a father figure to me. How could I file a case against my own father? I agree that I was at fault by not justifying myself earlier," explained Kartik.

"I have understood that. Anything else that you would like to tell me?" Shalini said and looked at him for the first time. He was wearing a cap that day and his head was bent. There was something different about his appearance. She suddenly realized that he had shaved off his dear moustache.

"Please forgive me," he said. Shalini did not reply. Maybe she was trying to find an answer to that question.

"Shalu, do you know what my friends told me when they saw my new look?" Kartik looked up and without waiting for an answer, he came closer and continued, "They said that *'Bihar ne Sindh ke liye apni moonchhe kurban kar di.'*

Though Shalini seemed to be lost, she was absorbing every word. Kartik asked if she knew who Shatrughan Sinha was. The last thing Shalini had expected during such a tense moment was the sudden reference to a Bollywood hero. She nodded and looked at Kartik's face without the moustache. He looked different – younger and cuter.

"He is a Bihari," Kartik said.

"I know that; in fact, everyone knows that. So?"

"Do you know who his wife is?"

"Must be some Biharan," Shalini said sarcastically.

"Yes exactly, she became a Biharan after marriage, but before that she was a Sindhi."

Shalini chose to keep quiet. Kartik immediately sat on the floor, took her hand in his and said, "I want to be your Shatrughan Sinha."

"What a way to say that!"

And suddenly Shalini had the same tingling feeling all over again.

Epilogue

"**K**artik, tea is ready. Come lets have it, or else the kids will wake up and then, you know Sankalp will not allow us to have anything," Shalini called out for her husband Kartik on a Sunday morning. They were parents of two young ones – a five-year-old daughter Kalash, and a one-and-a-half year old son Sankalp.

It was their tenth marriage anniversary on the 12th of November 2014, the same date when they committed to each other twelve years ago. It was one of the rare mornings when the children were not up yet and Shalini and Kartik could spend some time alone. They were getting nostalgic over a cup of tea while discussing their ten years of marriage. They were reminded of the umpteen number of fights they used to have during their courtship. Suddenly, they remembered the day when they had fought on the streets of Pusa over a small matter.

It was a day like any other summer day and there they were fighting again, and yes, as usual over a non-issue. However, this time, it was on the streets of Pusa. Pusa is a beautiful area in Delhi, where not fights, but romance should flourish.

Kartik was going to drop Shalini at Rajendar Nagar bus stop on her Scooty one Friday evening. They would take almost forty-five minutes and sometimes even an hour to complete the twenty-minute drive. During this extra time, they would talk about everything on earth. Both of them had strong opinions.

While Kartik used his maturity and the good head on his shoulders when he was putting forth his opinion, Shalini was basically driven by her emotions. The conversation would usually end in a short-lived fight because of their different stands on the same matter. It was short lived because even though they had different opinions on a given issue, their love for each other outdid the love for their opinions. They would make up as fast as they initiated the opinion war, as they called it.

That day it was a very different topic: casteism. For a young couple, who had been going around for about two years and who were already engaged with their families' acceptance, it was a very unusual topic.

The reason for the topic was that while Kartik was a Brahmin, Shalini only knew that she was Sindhi. Kartik had requested her to find out what her caste was and she had been adamant that now it should not be a cause for concern as they loved each other and even their parents had accepted their relationship.

Kartik then disclosed that he had lied to his parents saying that even Shalini was a Brahmin and that is why his parents had no problem in accepting her into the family. Stunned, Shalini had told Kartik to stop the Scooty.

"But why?" Kartik had asked.

"I said, please stop," she had said again.

"Okay, here we are, tell me what is it?" he had responded.

Shalini had got down and asked him why he had lied to his parents. "Is it because you also believe in the caste system?"

Kartik had assured Shalini that it did not matter to him but his parents were the kind of people to whom it mattered a lot. However, the fact had remained that she had not even known her caste.

Shalini had explained that for a girl born and brought up in a metro, caste was of little consequence and that her parents had never even discussed this matter, so the topic had never crossed her mind.

However, she had been feeling worried about something else. "We cannot start our life together by lying to our parents."

Kartik had been quick to realize that Shalini was getting emotional. He had assured Shalini that he would tell his parents the truth once she found out her caste. She had not responded and had sat down on a rock.

Kartik had held her hand, and had added, "I know what you are thinking. Do you know you are my life and I want to make you my wife?"

Immediately they had burst out laughing.

"Kartik, you are a very bad *shaayar*," she had said.

"Maybe, but I can make you laugh and that is what matters," he had declared. Shalini had blushed.

"See, I can make you blush too," he had winked.

Shalini had laughed again, but had said, "I cannot live without you."

"I know, my love, please don't worry. We will be together very soon," he had assured her.

In the meantime, they had reached a cold drink shop where they had shared a bottle. Their heads had cooled a bit and Shalini had agreed that for his sake she would ask her father about their caste. "However, I personally do not believe in this and would ask you not to pay attention to such things for our future family."

She had been sure that Kartik's parents were those kind of people, but her love, Kartik, definitely was mature enough to agree with her. The fight which had seemingly died down had resurfaced with this final remark.

Kartik had said, "Why not? I will definitely look for a Brahmin match for my children."

Shalini had been taken aback. She had not taken it well and had responded that she would never allow that to happen and would allow them to marry whoever they chose.

Kartik had immediately interrupted her, "When our parents have accepted our choice, even I will allow them the same freedom, but if they request us to find them a suitable match I will go for a Brahmin."

Shalini's anger had flared up and she had immediately retorted, "I will get them married off to one of my friend's children if that be the case." After a pause, she had added, "You know all my friends, tell me, who you think fits the bill as prospective in-laws for our prospective children?"

They had both voted for Raavi and Mohak. They were of the same wavelength. Although they had been married for two years, Raavi and Mohak had not had kids. So Shalini had answered, "Before you can take back your words, let's make it final."

Impulsive by nature, she had immediately called up Raavi and put forward the proposal of getting their children married with each others'. Raavi could not control herself and laughed out loud. She even told Mohak about the proposal while holding the phone. Shalini had put the mobile on loudspeaker so that Kartik would have no doubts about the finalization of the proposal. Gaining back her senses, Raavi, who had been laughing, promised that she would be the happiest if that happens. So, the proposal was finalized. Kartik and Shalini also patched up and Kartik dropped her home and went off.

Shalini was startled back to the present when Kartik asked her for some more tea and and asked her that since it had been ten years, what did she think of the proposal now?

Both of them burst into laughter. Shalini even fell off her chair and Kartik laughed out so loud that the kids woke up. Any guesses what the reason behind their laughter could be.

Yes, of course, they were thinking about the fact that while they had a daughter and a son, Raavi and Mohak had two daughters who were older to their own children. So Sankalp, being the youngest, had three elder didis. They were also thinking about how immature they were at that time. "Not that we have grown up much," Shalini said sheepishly.

But, before they could have more fun, both the children came running and planted themselves comfortably on the laps of their parents. Shalini smiled at Kartik and Kartik held her hand and kissed her, "Happy anniversary, my dear Shalu."

A note from the author

Iam writing this note with two intensions in mind. It is strange though that my 'two-point agenda' has a striking similarity with the two-point agenda of the female protagonist in the book.

The first point is that I firmly believe in the fact that when a man is educated, only he is educated; while when a woman is given education, she passes on the same to her entire family.

If we give our daughter the freedom to learn, to choose her career, to become what she wants to, let me assure you she will never let us down. I agree with the slogan initiated by our revered Prime Minister Shri Narendra Modi, *"Beti bachao, beti padhao."*

The second point I had in mind while writing this book was *"Zabaria Shaadi".* My husband told me about one of his friends who had forcibly been married off to a lady – a concept that existed a few years ago in areas of Bihar and Jharkhand.

I did my research and was shocked to read real-life incidents revolving around zabaria shaadi. What followed is the book: *Love Forever @ Rajpath.*

The concept of zabaria shaadi still exists in parts of central India. Google made me realize that many court cases revolving around zabaria shaadi are pending for years now. There have been instances where the newly-wed forced brides were not accepted by their husbands, and none other was willing to accept the girl in question, ruling out the possibilities of remarriage. On the other hand, there were cases where due to the clout of the girl's family, the husband allowed her to stay in the house, but did not keep any relation with her, and in a few cases remarried too.

I believe that this form of marriage is a consequence of the age-old evil practice of dowry. Unfortunately, of late, the demand for dowry has increased to such an extent that it can leave families destitute. The moment this evil practice is stopped, it will bring about an end to many crimes against women.

The book touches another sensitive topic: unavailability of public urinals, especially for women. When a person of the stature of our Prime Minister emphasized on the construction of public urinals while addressing the nation for the first time from the Red Fort on Independence Day, it made quite a few eyebrows go up. Many news channels also carried out full length discussions on how, till now, no Prime Minister had ever delivered a speech at such a grass-root level. To me, it was *bang on* the root cause of many molestation and rape cases. With a few big private companies joining in the endeavour, as Public Private Partnership and as a CSR activity, presumably the solution to these problems will be just round the corner.